BEST FRIENDS AND
FERRY TALES

A GREENSEA ISLAND ADVENTURE

JULIE FARLEY

FOG HOUSE
PRESS

For the lovers of Greensea

GREENSEA GAZETTE

Dear Islanders,

We're all still recovering from the Fourth of July parade—a spectacle none of us will ever forget. Apollo Bakeshop and Salty Cedar Distillery accidentally double-booked the same flatbed truck, and with no time to sort it out, they ended up sharing the ride. Picture Apollo's candy-striped bakers handing out ferry-shaped sugar cookies and Salty Cedar's scantily clad bartenders handing out mini-bottles of their new juniper gin. The float's popularity was off the charts—but Mayor Nickerbottom was not amused. Thankfully, the Salty Cedar folk only gave their (delicious) concoction to islanders who could show them a valid ID.

Speaking of sweet treats and beverages...The Royal Wedding is upon us! Jac Sherman is marrying the Johnny Nickel! Roll out the white carpet. Bring out the lilies. Polish all the silver. But please, whatever you do, don't throw rice! It's not actually dangerous for our birds but it is a mess to clean up and is slippery on the sidewalks! With all our island lawyers, Greensea does not need the extra liability. How about flower petals, bubbles, or biodegradable confetti? And for heaven's sake, do not whatever you do, release balloons. We don't need to explain why, do we?

And finally, a note from Mayor Nickerbottom:

> While the city council appreciates the quiet resistance with the entry of the garden gnomes float in the parade, the law has the final word, no matter how much support you've drummed up. City ordinance 3.7.8 clearly states that plastic yard ornaments may not be placed on any public piece of property, no matter how festive their attire is or what size they may be. NO. MORE. GNOMES. They will be confiscated, placed in a secure city office, and not returned—ever.

Well then. The mayor is not messing around.

xoxo,

GG

CHAPTER ONE

OLIVER

"Here, take a sip of water."

Feathers fall onto the seat as I pull the water bottle out of Daisy's bag.

"What do you have in there? Did you bring a pet parakeet?" I'm almost afraid to hear her answer.

"It's my boa," she replies with a giggle.

Of course it is. Only Daisy Bennett would bring a boa in her carry-on to Greensea Island.

She settles in, gripping the armrest as sunlight streams through the airplane window, catching her emerald-green eyes, making them shimmer.

"Thank you for coming to get me, Ollie. You're the best best friend's brother in the entire world."

The title "best friend's brother" stings a little and feels like a fence I'm not allowed to climb.

Daisy hiccups. "Oops, excuse me." She puts her hands over her mouth.

I stepped off my first flight to San Francisco and

spotted Daisy standing at the gate with her black hair piled into a messy bun, wearing quilted pants, a denim vest, and a white tank—classic Daisy. I knew something was amiss when she slurred hello. It only took her a minute to confess she'd taken a gummy made of ashwagandha and passionflower that she'd picked up at Burning Man along with some moon tea—whatever that is—to help her relax on our flight.

"I'm just nervous," she says for the twenty-fifth time.

"I know you are," I repeat, also for the twenty-fifth time. "But your mom was wrong. Nothing 'significant' is going to happen on this flight."

"My mom's always right. She knew when my first tooth was going to fall out." Daisy's face is serious like she's giving the closing arguments at a murder trial.

I turn my head and share my rebuttal. "Probably because you were six years old, and it was wiggling in your mouth."

"She predicted the Red Sox would break the Curse of the Bambino." Her bangles jingle with emphasis.

Statistically, that was bound to happen after 86 years and millions of dollars sunk into the team. I don't bother pointing it out.

"And she predicted the temperatures at last year's Burning Man would exceed 100 degrees." She delivers her final argument.

I choke out a laugh. "Is it ever under 100 degrees?"

Daisy's mom is not the next Nostradamus. But my job is to be a reassuring companion and not to argue about her mom's status as a prophet.

"I'm here to keep you safe. Sit back and close your eyes." I pat her knee.

Jac told me, *Fly down, keep Daisy calm, fly back—*

easy! I said *yes*, knowing I could work on the plane. As it's turning out, this is more therapeutic reassurance and less client work. But I'm always quick to volunteer to help Daisy in whatever capacity necessary.

The captain's voice crackles overhead. "Ladies and gentlemen, in accordance with FAA regulations, please buckle your seatbelts and stow all electronic devices for takeoff. Place any handheld devices in airplane mode."

Daisy ignores the announcement and reaches into her bag and checks something on her phone.

"Dais, time to place it in airplane mode."

"Relax, Mr. Rule Follower," she says like that's a bad thing. "I'm checking the turbulence tracker one more time, and then I'll turn my phone off."

She takes a screenshot and sticks her phone in her seat pocket. What the hell is a turbulence tracker? Are there really people who keep track of how many bumps there might be on a plane ride?

"The first four minutes will be moderately bumpy, followed by 17 minutes of light turbulence before we go through the atmospheric river separating San Francisco from Seattle," she says.

"You got all that from your app?"

The plane pulls away from the gate.

"Sure did."

"Try not to count the bumps. It will make them worse."

"Knowledge is power. I thought you'd understand that better than anyone Mr. Numbers." She gives a wink with my new moniker. "If I'm prepared, I'm not as scared."

"Flight attendants, prepare for departure," the captain's voice bellows.

Daisy assumes her white knuckled hold on the armrests.

"Breathe," I whisper into her ear and peel her hand off the armrest before she cuts off the circulation to her fingertips as we roar down the runway. I keep her hand in mine as the plane ascends out of the Bay Area. Her hand's warm—a tad clammy—and soft. Like it's meant to rest in mine.

"Look." I pull my hand away and do my best to distract her. "There's the Bay Bridge. Mount Diablo. All your favorite haunts."

She rests her head back on the seat, but I see her eyes move to the left.

A bell sounds signaling we've reached 10,000 feet.

"From the flight deck, you may now use our complimentary WiFi service. Flight attendants will be around with our beverage service when we've reached a comfortable cruising altitude. We expect to hit some turbulence as we cross through a bit of weather. We may turn the seatbelt sign on if we need to and have our flight attendants return to their seats. It is a federal regulation to follow and comply with all safety requests."

"See, everything's fine. We made it through the dangerous part."

"It's all dangerous, Oliver. And my mom is never wrong."

I should be diving into my client's Q2 financials, but keeping Daisy from spiraling is more urgent.

"We've got quite the weekend ahead—wedding events start bright and early tomorrow."

"Really? Do they?" She bites the corner of her lip.

"They do," I answer, unable to imagine how she hasn't analyzed the itinerary for the entire weekend. I mean, I've mapped it to the minute to make sure I can still log all my miles for my triathlon training.

Daisy keeps her head back like we're on a roller coaster progressing up a hill.

"I'm sure whatever Jac has planned for this wedding will be dreamy. My mom says this wedding's the real deal."

I nod. Daisy's mom is right about that. Jac and Johnny are for real. Jac's first wedding ended in a quick divorce when her husband emptied their bank account and left her a letter stating he was off to find himself. And while the tabloid magazines aren't giving this second marriage much of a chance, each gossip rag guessing when the legendary Johnny Nickel will grow bored with his kindergarten teacher bride, I'm betting my sister will hook him forever.

Daisy signals the flight attendant, asking for a glass of wine before we reach the atmospheric river. She opens her tray table and drums her fingers while she waits. I can't imagine what she'd be like if she hadn't taken the concoction from Burning Man.

She doesn't waste any time when the flight attendant hands her the wine; she drinks it like she's been entered in a chugging contest, even slamming it down on the tray table just as the seatbelt sign comes on.

The plane shakes, and her whole body tenses with the first set of bumps.

"Where'd you get this ring?" I rub the large oval grey-black stone on her index finger.

"It's a mood ring that I found in a thrift store in Joshua Tree."

I don't believe in mood rings, but I glance at it anyway and wish it would turn green.

"I've never been to Joshua Tree." I'm not a fan of the desert heat, so I've always skipped the popular spot.

"It's one of my energy vortexes."

She covers her hand over her ring and takes a quick look. The color doesn't change.

"Your what now?"

"A place where my vibration sings," she says, like it's the most obvious thing in the world. My energy only hums in front of a whiteboard or a daily planner.

The plane shakes. The engines soar. Daisy digs her nails into her palms, and I squeeze her hand in mine. Jac failed to mention Operation-Bring-Daisy-to-Greensea would be so hands-on.

"It's okay. We're moving through changing air currents, and the plane's adjusting. Pretend we're driving on a highway with lots of potholes. Planes don't crash because of turbulence."

She looks straight ahead. Then out the window. And then straight ahead again.

"How do you know so much about airplanes? Other than looking like you were in Top Gun, you're not an expert." She shakes her head.

I roll my eyes. Close-cropped blond hair? Check. Aviators? Check. Bomber jacket? No way.

She reaches into her purse and grabs another gummy. More feathers fly out.

"How many of those are you supposed to take?" I try to hide any judgment, but I'm certain I crinkled my nose.

"They didn't come with a recommended daily dose, but I need them right now while I'm stuck up here at 36,000 feet in a tin can hurling through the air."

She tries to chase the gummy down with the dregs in her paper cup of wine.

"Let me see the package."

"There isn't a package. Just a plastic bag. Igor made them, and I trust him with my life."

"Igor?"

The mere mention of the name Igor calls up images of a bearded seven-foot-tall bodybuilder. Not a crafter of pharmaceuticals.

"Yes, he's my desert buddy. I even helped make his wedding official."

His wedding? I look at Daisy's empty ring finger and let out a sigh of relief.

"It's fine, Ollie, I pinky promise." She holds out her pinky and reaches down to grab mine off my lap. So much touching. But to my relief, she closes her eyes, and I can get some work done.

Juggling wedding duties with my work responsibilities and personal goals gives me heartburn, but taking days off from any of my pursuits would stress me out even more. As I listen to Daisy's baby sighs, I notice her ring is turning more grey than black.

Progress. I'll take it.

The bustle of the flight attendants preparing for arrival wakes Daisy as we circle the Space Needle and make our final descent to the airport.

I lean across her seat to get a better view out the window—I can't resist looking at Greensea from the air. Watching the ferries run back and forth. The Ferris wheel. I can practically smell the sea air. Daisy's gentle breath on my cheek rearranges the numbers in my brain. Focus, Oliver.

"There's our house." I point to our cove and a blob that resembles the Sherman house. "And Dave's oyster farm over there." I point toward Bungalow Bay.

Daisy looks and then sighs. "Greensea makes me happy."

"Really? Why?" I ask.

"Every time I visit, it's like I'm wrapped up in a weighted blanket with everything taken care of. It's the only place I feel that way." She turns her head, and a curl falls onto her cheek, tempting me to tuck it behind her ear, but I ball my fists up instead.

"Then you should spend more time here. Maybe it's another personal energy vortex," I say in an almost whisper.

She shrugs as the landing gear goes down.

"See, there's the runway. We're almost down."

Daisy's right foot is pushing an invisible brake pedal with all her might while we approach the ground.

"Aaannnd we made it." The engines roar to a stop. "Nothing significant took place."

She's quiet, taking deep breaths. "Yoooou're my hero, Ollie." The effects of her Burning Man gummy have not dwindled, but I don't mind being Daisy Bennett's hero.

CHAPTER TWO

OLIVER

"Enjoy the wedding, Mr. Sherman," the flight attendant says with a knowing smile as we step off the plane.

Right. That.

Sometimes I forget—we've all become tabloid regulars. I didn't think they'd care about Jac's third brother, but they care about everything, including the kind of milk we buy (organic and pasteurized; we're not monsters). The Daily Mail even ran a feature on the *Royal Shermans of Greensea.*

Everyone wants a glimpse of the fairytale: a rockstar marrying a normal, small-town girl. The third brother and whatever Daisy is to me—that's third-page news, but they still want it. And the flight attendants are eating it up.

I hook an arm around Daisy to move her along a little faster since she's walking like she's trudging through quicksand. At her rate, we'll never make it through the terminal.

When we get to baggage claim, I lean her against a wall next to a rack of brochures about whale watching.

"Stay here. I'll grab your bag."

"It's purple and has a bell tied to it," she says with a dazed smile.

That tracks. I could have picked it out of a lineup without any instruction.

Judging from the size of her luggage, I wouldn't be surprised if she has her entire closet with her. Or a Burning Man starter kit. I pull up the handle on the suitcase—sturdy, not one of those flimsy ones—when an idea hits me.

"Get on," I say.

She turns her head and looks at me.

"On the suitcase?"

"Yep, sit on it and lean back. I'm going to pull you."

She does as I say, and I tilt the suitcase back and pull her through the throngs of people like she's a parade float. Daisy giggles and rings the bell as we go, even throwing in a royal wave. Heads turn and a few cameras flash, but it's all in good fun.

As promised, Arianna is waiting for us at the curb. Her eyes widen when she sees us.

"Oh my gosh!" Arianna looks between me and my makeshift carnival ride. "Are you... is she okay?"

I ease Daisy off her perch. "She's fine."

Daisy peers up at Arianna. "Whooo's this?" she asks before stumbling into the backseat.

"Daisy, meet my friend, Arianna."

Arianna cocks her head and lifts one eyebrow. "Friend?"

I ignore her and hoist Daisy's bags into the trunk.

Girlfriend seems premature—we've only been

hanging out for a little over a month, and my heart and my brain keep sending me mixed messages.

Plus one seems cold.

Friend is appropriate.

"I'm going to take the ferry over with Daisy to make sure she gets there okay." The last thing this wedding needs is a bridesmaid lost at sea.

Arianna peeks in the rearview mirror. Daisy's got the window open in the backseat, leaning her head out to get some air like she's a golden retriever.

"She's going to see Johnny Nickel in that condition?"

"Johnny and I are besties!" Daisy giggles.

Arianna lets out a humph. "And when do I get to meet Johnny?" She glares at me, and I wish she'd keep her eyes on the road.

"You're coming over tomorrow evening for the bachelor and bachelorette party."

"Perfect. I'll have time to ask him some questions," she says.

"Questions?" I ask.

"Oh, you know, get acquainted." Her hands are flying wildly, and I'm half convinced I should take the wheel.

"Dress code?" she asks.

"Casual," I say, and make a mental note to check the itinerary.

She rolls to a stop at the ferry terminal loading zone. Daisy eases out of the car and, while I retrieve her bags, props herself against a telephone pole like she's completed a marathon instead of a short flight.

"Bye, Daisy. Feel better!" Arianna calls from her open window.

The trunk's hardly closed before she peels off.

"Sorry," says Daisy. "Shedoesnotlikeme."

As Arianna's car disappears into traffic, I exhale hard. I don't know what, or who, Arianna likes.

We approach the ferry ticket booth, and Daisy leans in with a grin for the attendant. "May I gift you something in exchange for a ticket?" she asks, rummaging through her bag.

The ticket seller blinks, caught between confusion and curiosity.

I quietly slide my credit card across the counter. "Two for Greensea, please," I say, as Daisy triumphantly pulls out a hat knit with every color of the rainbow, holding it up like a treasure.

The ticket seller shakes their head.

I take the tickets and hold the back of Daisy's vest, leading her into the terminal. "People can't take goods for things that cost actual money."

She sighs. "So traditional of you, Ollie. You'd be surprised at the power of a gift economy." She giggles again, and I walk her onto the ferry.

Part of me is afraid her theory about the gift economy is something she believes even when she's sober and not just when she's high on passionflower.

"How about some food?" I ask.

"Yessss." A dribble of drool escapes her mouth. I'll get a napkin too.

She plops herself into a booth next to a window with a view of the Ferris wheel still decked out in red, white, and blue.

I step into the galley and grab a beer for myself, a pretzel with cheese for Daisy, and a large bottle of water. All the while, I keep one eye on her from the checkout line, rushing through the payment in case she makes a move to get up.

"I don't drink out of plastics," she moans as I hand her the water bottle.

"You need to drink something, so give it up for now. You can go back to your virtues tomorrow when the gummies wear off."

I place the pretzel on the table and slide it in front of her. "Eat."

"I'm sorry my mom was wrong, and nothing happened on our flight. You had to go all that way for no reason." She sighs.

No harm done. I never thought anything was going to happen. Escorting Daisy to Greensea was an easy way to help Jac and not an unpleasant way to spend a day. I can't imagine how scared she would have been if she were alone, or how she would have gotten through SeaTac by herself. I didn't mind being her co-pilot today.

I text Jac to give her a heads up.

> Oliver: On the ferry with Daisy. She took one too many gummies on the plane.

> Jac: You're the best brother in the universe. Thank you so much! Dad made a charcuterie board so that should sop up some of it.

> Oliver: Meet me in the terminal so I can turn around and get back on the ferry.

> Jac: Roger Dodger!

Daisy rips off a piece of pretzel—my favorite ferry treat—and scoops up the cheese. When some trails down her chin, I hand her a napkin like I'm passing a secret note. Somehow, she smears the cheese across her face, so I reach over and wipe it off myself. She tilts her head down and presses her lips to my finger. Soft. Like she doesn't even know she's doing it.

"Thank you, Ollie. Thank you for everything."

And then she puts her head against the window and closes her eyes. But I can't move.

Her lips against my skin recall a memory that's been living rent-free in the back of my mind—the memory of our secret, stolen kiss from years ago.

It's one of those moments I sometimes wish we could erase—and yet, somehow, I simultaneously want to commemorate it every single day. Jac and Daisy had just graduated from college and were spending one last summer holiday on Greensea before launching their new lives in San Francisco. Daisy asked to join me on a run—said she wasn't confident on the trails and didn't want to get lost. I told her to meet me in the driveway—bright and early—before the heat set in.

The forest was quiet, still waking up. Dew clung to the leaves, and our footsteps were the only sound as we climbed the trail. When we reached the clearing at the top of the trail, something white caught our eyes—an albino deer, glimmering as it stood against the lush green backdrop like it had stepped out of a dream.

Daisy gasped. I wrapped her in a hug to quiet her so we wouldn't scare it off. She looked up at me with those wide green eyes, and kissing her felt like the most natural thing in the world. So I did.

I can still remember the softness of her lips, how the forest seemed to come alive with the songs of birds the moment our mouths met. When we finally pulled away, I apologized, stumbling over my words. But Daisy just smiled and said, "It was meant to be."

And that was it. We never spoke of it again, not even once—despite all the times I've seen her since.

Unfortunately, the kiss broke the number one rule of the Sherman Family: No tomfoolery with your siblings' friends. In a house with three boys and one girl, Mom and Dad had no choice but to put it into writing. The first incident happened when Jac was six. Betty O'Brien came over for a playdate and put her bunny crackers in Dave's cup—like, the cup he used at Little League. She thought it was a bowl. Mrs. O'Brien freaked out, called the doctor to make sure her daughter wouldn't get any sexually transmitted diseases, told GG Mom was serving snacks in x-rated objects, and warned Mom and Dad to keep her boys and all their parts away from her daughter. Thus 'no tomfoolery' was born. It became more serious as we got older when ring pops and fake proposals were involved.

My brain rationalizes the feelings in my heart away—this small peck while I removed cheese didn't break any rules.

Daisy snores as the ferry cruises into Grays Bay.

I stand up and get ready to grab all of Daisy's things. "Dais, get up."

She doesn't stir as the familiar announcement comes on, reminding passengers to disembark the ferry in the manner they got on. I never really understood the need for the reminder—until last week, when they had to call the Coast Guard because someone left their car on the ferry. Turns out after seventeen years of walking onto the ferry as a foot passenger, Mr. Harris' muscle memory took over. He'd completely forgotten he'd driven his oldest son to the airport that morning. He just strolled off as usual—only realizing something was amiss when Mrs. Harris wasn't waiting at the curb. That's when it hit him: his car was still in the hull.

I nudge Daisy's arm. She wipes her hand across her face and opens her eyes. She stands up, a little wobbly, and throws her bag on her shoulder.

"Jac's meeting us in the terminal." I place my hand on the small of her back and guide her to the exit.

"That last gummy wiped me out." She's less goofy, more exhausted right now.

"The wine probably didn't help."

"Truth," she says.

She looks down and moves toward the ferry doors, and I link my arm through hers as we walk to the ferry terminal. Her curls—scented with patchouli, sandalwood, and a touch of vanilla, like incense laced with a hint of nervous sweat—tickle my nose.

She stops as we step into the terminal, looks up, and leans toward me. I don't move a muscle as she parts her lips and presses them gently against mine.

Time catches. I want to kiss her back, but we're surrounded by fellow islanders and familial expectations. Jac and the rest of the clan would string me up like a steelhead and let bald eagles feast on my guts because now we're in rule-breaking territory.

"Dais!" I choke out.

"What?" She pulls away and hiccups.

"You can't..." I shake my head. "Just kiss me!"

"But you're my Ollie." She laughs like that explains everything.

I have to get her to Jac before I forget how to do the right thing.

We round the corner, and Jac runs up to us, wrapping

Daisy in a hug for their bestie reunion. Thank goodness she wasn't ten seconds earlier.

"I'm getting married!" Jac screams into Daisy's hair. She lets go of Daisy and gives me a quick hug. "Thank you again."

I nod and return to the ferryboat with tantalizing thoughts of Daisy and kiss number three.

CHAPTER THREE

DAISY

Everything is moving in slow motion, like I'm in a dream or underwater—maybe trapped inside a lava lamp. Even though I'm on solid ground, my legs are still doing a wobbly ferry dance.

Oliver, with his close-cropped sandy blond hair, was just standing in front of me. His green eyes looked serious, and all I could think about were his lips—cool and minty like his gum. I couldn't resist kissing him.

His lips felt every bit as lovely as they did during our first kiss years ago, only this time—there was no magical albino deer in the meadow while we were running—just us and hundreds of ferry riders.

Thankfully, he pulled away, and Jac wrapped me in a hug before my brain could spiral any deeper into thoughts of her off-limits brother. Part of me has been pining over Oliver ever since he helped Jac move into her dorm room —the same day she loudly announced to the entire floor that, due to family history, her brothers were officially off-limits to her friends. She didn't want to risk losing any of us in a custody battle over the family group chat. The unintended consequence of her proclamation was that Oliver became forbidden fruit and the object of my secret desires.

"Let's get you in the car," Jac says, guiding me to the doors of the ferry terminal.

"It was bumpy, and I was nervous. And my mom was wrong! Nothing happened." I focus on enunciating every word, concentrating as I put one foot in front of the other on our way to the car.

"Hello, Daisy!" Johnny, dapper as ever in a pale green sweater and rockstar ripped jeans, opens the car door for me. His British accent is so jolly it makes me giggle, but in fairness, everything is making me snicker right now.

"Ollie was sooooo nice to fly with me. Thank you for sending him!"

"Anytime! The Sherman brothers are happy to do anything for you!" Jac reaches over the front seat and squeezes my knee.

I sigh. "He's the nicest Sherman boy. He's my albino deer."

"What's an albino deer?" asks Johnny.

"It's an all-white deer with blue eyes and a pink nose that lives in the Grand Greensea Forest. Island lore says you'll come into good fortune if you see it," explains Jac.

I put my head back on the seat. I could use some of the deer's good fortune right now.

We pull out of the parking lot and cruise down Main Street. A banner stretches across, fluttering in the breeze with a cheerful message: *Ferry Ever After: Johnny + Jac.* Floral garlands spiral up every lamppost, bursting with soft pinks and wild greens. The bakery window is a dreamy display of tulle, sugar flowers, and towering wedding cakes. And over at *Between the Covers*, the bookstore has arranged its window with a heart-shaped stack of romance novels—love stories stacked on love stories. Greensea is dripping with wedding bliss.

I glance down at my mood ring—green. Calm and peaceful. Maybe Oliver was right, and Greensea is another vortex for me. But even with all the serene scenery, Igor's treats have exhausted me, and I can't help but close my eyes.

"Wakey-wakey!" Jac tickles me under my chin when we arrive.

For the second time this evening—at least that I'm aware of—I wipe drool off my face. Jac lends me an arm, and we walk to the house. My favorite brick path leads right to the front door of the Shermans' brown shingled ranch.

The house is quiet. Two lamps burn on the kitchen island, highlighting Tom's legendary charcuterie board with *Welcome Daisy* spelled out in olives.

I try to remember if my dad or mom ever put food out for me when I came home to visit. Our house had warmth —but the herbal kind. Homemade kombucha. A stick of palo santo on the windowsill.

The Sherman's house is usually filled with people— brothers causing a ruckus, always someone making food in the kitchen. The laughter and ribbing of siblings is what I missed growing up. It's a Nancy Meyers movie on steroids, and this week will be like a never-ending run of *Father of the Bride*. Tonight is quiet, but it's the calm before the storm.

I pull out a stool and make a cracker sandwich with brie and fig jam.

"I have to thank your dad for this masterpiece. Where is he?" I ask between bites.

"Mom and Dad are out in the yard in the RV living their best life." Jac points outside.

Somehow, I didn't even notice it when we came down the driveway. Chalk that up to the gummies and the low light after sunset. Barb and Tom, Jac's parents, are preparing to hit the road in their RV after the wedding. Jac and Johnny will make the Sherman house their residence whenever they're on Greensea.

Johnny's a rockstar, but this place is more coastal grandmother chic. The more I get to know Johnny, the more he gives English gentleman—classic literature and crossword puzzles—and not hard drugs and parties.

"You'll see Dad tomorrow morning," Jac says.

"I'll take your bags downstairs." Johnny, the giant pop star, acts like my personal butler.

"Thanks!" I take another cracker and cheese.

"Johnny and I are in the primary." Jac smiles and giggles, picking an olive from the W in the center of the board. "You'll have my room all to yourself."

"No separate beds until the wedding night?" I ask with a wink.

Johnny returns after depositing my bags. "She's making me sleep somewhere else the night before the wedding. I have something special planned for the boys."

"And all the girls are staying here for a good old-fashioned sleepover!" Jac cheers.

"Until then, she's all mine." Johnny plants a kiss on Jac's lips.

"Get a room!" I finish my last bite of a cracker and take that as my cue to mosey down to Jac's room. Falling asleep tonight will not be a problem.

———

The house is buzzing when I wake up. Barb's unmistakable giggle echoes through the ceiling. The sweet, buttery scent of pancakes drifts down through the vents, enveloping me in a hug. Comfort food sounds magical right now.

I grab my phone from the nightstand. My heart races. Seventeen notifications.

Bluebird Coffee rejected the changes I made to their logo. A dozen *thanks but no thanks* emails from other potential clients. A text from my landlord reminding me that rent is due, and no, I cannot clean the laundry room for him in exchange for a discount. And Adam, my plus one for the wedding, sent a selfie from his tent in a far corner of Alaska as he waits to see the Northern Lights.

I toss my phone down like it's radioactive and pull the covers up around my neck.

I can't believe Adam picked the Northern Lights over being my date for the wedding. Even though I decided we were better off as friends after our failed attempt at dating —I chase meaning, and he chases experience—it stings. It would have been nice to have a strong arm on the dance floor and a suit jacket to borrow when the sun went down. The sixteen other messages hurt too. They're just not as personal as Adam's.

I steel my resolve and remember I'm putting my San Francisco life on hold for the wedding. The real world can wait while I stand next to Jac as she gets married. I'm certain the bill collectors and nonexistent job prospects will still be there when the wedding is over.

I'm on Greensea now—in Jac's bedroom where time seems frozen between high school and our college years.

A faded pennant hangs on the wall and Polaroids of our best college friends smile at me like good times still exist.

Time to focus on the present moment and the sweet smells of breakfast.

The bedroom door creaks open, and I stuff my worries under the covers.

"Morning, sleepyhead," says Jac as she plops down on the bed. Her skin looks like it's been polished with diamond dust. Her teeth are as white as can be, and I think I can see my reflection in her glossy hair. Jac is radiant.

"I'm getting married soon!" She squeals and bounces on the bed. It's like she can hardly believe it. I mean the entire story is a fairy tale—or a ferry tale, as they're calling it. I couldn't be happier for my best friend, even if my reality is a little less sunny at the moment.

"What's up, buttercup?" asks Jac.

"Oh, just a little tired from traveling." I plaster a cheek-to-cheek smile on my face. "What's the plan for today?" I vaguely remember Oliver mentioning our packed schedule, but was confident I'd be able to roll with whatever it was once I arrived on Greensea.

"Mom's making breakfast, and then you and I are going to the spa with Tippy and Sylviane."

Tippy and Sylviane are dating Jac's brothers, Dave and Josh. I swear the Shermans welcome me like I'm the lost fifth sibling.

I throw my legs off the bed and get up reaching for a sweatshirt. There's a chill in the air on Greensea even in July.

"Duuuude!" yells Jac. She gets up close and looks under my arm. "You're going to need to shave that bush under your arms before the wedding."

I clamp my arms down to my sides.

"Can a razor even get through that? What the hell!"

"I've been letting myself go au naturel. It's so free-ing. You should try it. It's another way to shift the power equilibrium from men. I met this girl at Burning Man who sells natural deodorant rocks that neutralize the bacteria and she really sold me on the complete process."

To be honest, she didn't really sell me on it as much as she gave it to me for free.

"Well, that's great but I do not want that in my wedding pictures." Jac looks at me again. "Something could be living under there. I'm afraid to ask what your legs look like."

Yeah, she will not be happy when she sees them. I give her a guilty look.

"I'll call Glenda and give her a heads up before we head over."

"Glenda? Are we're going to see the good witch?"

"At Greensea Glam."

Of course. Everything has a cutesy name on the island.

"No need. I'll just pick up a razor at the drugstore." A full wax job at Greensea Glam will be pricey unless Glenda needs a new logo or something I can barter with my graphic design skills.

"Don't be ridiculous. It's my wedding and I don't trust Bic to get the job done."

I give Jac a half smile and she hits my arm. "Come on. Let's get some breakfast."

"Daisy!" croons Barb. She puts down her spatula and wraps me in a bear hug. Tom comes over and adds his embrace. Being around the Shermans means you always hit your eight hugs a day minimum. "We're so glad you're here!"

Barb and Tom are the consummate parents. They came to every parents' weekend in college dressed in all their spirit gear. Always took the entire gang to dinner. They support their kids in whatever they're doing. Making treasure maps? They're the first customers. Opening an oyster bar? They're back there shucking. Marrying a rockstar? They're learning all his lyrics.

Barb makes me a plate of pancakes and sets it at a place on the island.

"How are your parents?" Tom asks.

"Oh, they haven't changed much. They've been touring with a Joni Mitchell impersonator like it's 1972. They travel the country and go to all of her shows. Total throwback to their old festival days."

Part of me has been jealous of the whole family scene since the first time I met the Shermans, freshman year in college. I'm an only child who sometimes felt like a sidekick, as my parents lived out their hippie yearnings. Don't get me wrong; I loved going from festival to festival chasing my free bird dreams, and my friends were always jealous that I never had a curfew—or any rules, for that matter—but the kind of family you see in the movies—that's what I've always wanted.

"Love that for them," says Barb. "Now I want to know everything about you. How's work going? Oh, and I need all the deets, as they say, about your date to the wedding."

"Ummm, well…" It's all I can get out. Don't want to spill the beans right now.

Tom interrupts my stammering. "Barb, let the poor girl be. She had a long night, and she has plenty of time to get you caught up this week."

I shoot a smile of gratitude in Tom's direction and take a bite of a pancake slathering up the syrup.

"Barb! These are delicious." I practically moan. "What's your secret ingredient?"

"Nutmeg! I livestreamed the whole thing this morning!"

Jac rolls her eyes.

"I think you need a logo for your social media sites," I say.

Barb puts down her spatula and looks at me. "That's just what I need! Any chance you have time to make one for me? I'll pay the going rate."

My going rate may be the plate of pancakes sitting in front of me. "For you, free!"

"Dais, you can't just give things away. Oliver mentioned you tried to barter with the ferry attendant. Are you getting paid for your gigs?" Jac's wearing her best I-know-the-dog-didn't-eat-your-homework teacher face.

I laugh and shoo the suggestion away. "Don't worry about me!" I turn toward Barb. "I'll work on some ideas for you while I'm here."

She sidles up next to me and gives me another squeeze.

"You girls better get over to Glenda's!"

GREENSEA GAZETTE

Islanders,

Since yours truly has exclusive access to all the wedding details, I'd like to introduce you to the important parties involved in this event.

Wedding Story

Jac (short for JacLynn) Sherman accidentally fell in love with (unbeknownst to her) the biggest pop star in the world, Johnny Nickel, while he was renting the Sherman family home, trying to escape the spotlight on our tiny island. Think accidental run-ins after showers, midnight snacks, and sudsy kisses. Their love story was fraught with stolen moments and paparazzi, but true love prevailed, and we find ourselves ready to celebrate their wedding.

Wedding Party

Oliver Sherman: Best man - Can always be "counted" on
Josh Sherman: Groomsman - (Official wedding grump)
Not happy about the influx of tourists
Dave Sherman: Groomsman - Speaks fluent sea creature
Daisy Bennett: Maid of Honor - No need to burn sage
when she's around because she'll set your chakras straight
with a touch of her hand
Sylviane DuPont: Bridesmaid - Bestselling author of cozy
whodunnits. Voted most likely to solve any wedding
mystery
Tippy Meadowcroft: Bridesmaid - Pickleball champ.
Pilates expert. No. 1 island gossip reporter. Fantastic girl-
friend and daughter...I could go on and on.
Sam Montgomery: Master of Ceremonies and Wedding
Officiant - Johnny's best mate and all-around good bloke

Family of the Bride and Groom

Barb Sherman: Mother of the Bride - TikTok cooking
sensation proudly sponsored by KitchenAid
Tom Sherman: Father of the Bride - Future RV captain
with a heart of gold
Anne Nickel: Mother of the Groom - Birthed a superstar.
You're welcome, world!

The wedding will take place aboard the retired MV
Tokitae—the Lummi name for the orcas, based on the
Chinook word meaning a nice day. Don't say you never
learned anything from GG!

Stay tuned for all the details you didn't know you needed!

xoxo,

GG

CHAPTER FOUR

DAISY

Jac doesn't waste a second questioning me as soon as we hop into her car.

"What's going on with you?" She locks the car doors for emphasis. "You're not going anywhere until you tell me."

"This is not the week to worry about me. It's your wedding. You're marrying the man of your dreams. Let's focus on that."

I roll down my window.

"Don't try to divert my attention that easily. Give me a quick rundown."

I sigh, realizing she will not let me off the hook, and it might be hard to escape from both her car and an island. "Work isn't as plentiful as I'd hoped."

I went out on my own last year and started a graphic design company. AI and other tools are making it unnecessary to hire a little guy like me, and the big players—well, they only want to work with the huge firms.

"Is there anything I can do to help?"

Jac's set for life now that she's marrying Johnny. There's no need for her to count crayons and clip coupons on her teacher's salary anymore, but I'm not about to live off my best friend's good fortune. I'll find my magic. Somehow.

"Nope, it's going to be fine. I need to find my groove, and I'm sure to be at my creative peak after this extravaganza." I laugh and turn on the music. Luckily, the universe is on my side as a Johnny Nickel song comes on and Jac can't help but sing instead of interrogating.

We let the sea air blow through our hair as we drive the gentle rolling hills of Greensea. Mother Nature got today right—sunny with a side of seventy degrees. There's always a taste of salt mingled with pine trees, no matter where you are on Greensea. It's a soothing balm for my soul. Being with Jac and the Shermans, plus the aura of Greensea, is what I need to find my footing again.

Greensea Glam is housed in a Cape Cod-style home in the center of Grays Bay. The white shingled exterior and shake roof give off coastal vibes as soon as you arrive.

We pull into the parking lot just as Tippy rides up on her bike.

"Greetings!" She puts down her kickstand and comes over to give us each a hug. Tippy reaches into a tote bag nestled in a basket on the front of her bike, takes out a sash that says "bride," and places it on Jac's shoulders.

"Don't want anyone to forget who you are!"

A car door closes behind us, and Sylviane appears.

"I'm so glad you made it okay!" Sylviane touches my shoulder before she takes a veil headband from behind her back and sets it atop Jac's head.

"Now you're all set!" exclaims Tippy.

Jac claps her hands and squeals—signature bride move. The four of us join hands and do a bridal party ring-around-the-rosie in the parking lot.

"Thank you guys for supporting me! This wedding is for keeps!"

"It better be or we will tank Johnny Nickel's career," says Tippy.

"As if you have that kind of power," replies Sylviane.

Sylviane and Jac walk toward the door while Tippy pulls my arm and slows me down.

"Hey, I got an anonymous tip that you were kissing Oliver in the ferry terminal last night," she whispers.

Oh, shit. I freeze. Jac's going to kill me. Why did I do that? My face warms thinking of the kiss and how out of it I was.

"I took a couple of ashwagandha gummies on the plane. I think I even kissed the pilot after we landed." I laugh it off and embellish with a white lie. Oliver's the only other one who knows the truth, and he won't tell.

There's no reason to let anyone else in on the secret that I compare every set of lips I kiss to Ollie's and have ached to feel them again since our first kiss years ago.

Sylviane turns around and looks at us. "What are you two whispering about back there?"

"Oh, nothing. Got an anonymous report that Daisy was a little off her rocker on the ferry last night."

Jac laughs. "She sure was! You should have seen her! She was calling Oliver her albino deer."

Hiding the truth is easier than I thought, but I wish I hadn't been such a mess. It would have helped to remember that news travels at lightning speed on this little island.

The interior of Greensea Glam is all white and

serene. Instrumental spa music plays in the background, and a fountain drips in the waiting area. The familiar scent of Palo Santo fills my nose. This place will no doubt calm my nerves, even if I'm worried all the work I need done will sully the place.

An older woman dressed in white scrubs and a name tag that reads Glenda greets us at the front desk.

"Who's ready for a wedding glow-up?" she asks, and we all raise our hands. "I hear someone needs some repair work before she gets polished."

I take a tiny step forward. "Guilty as charged."

"You three go that way." Glenda points to the right. "She's all mine." Her voice has the same vibe as a fairy tale witch about to pop me in the oven.

She leads me back to a separate room with strict instructions. "Take everything off and slide under the blanket. I'll be back in a jiff to assess this situation."

In San Francisco, I've never questioned the state of my hair. Who cares if I can braid my leg hair? But I'm punching myself for not thinking about it before I arrived on Greensea. I mean, I am at one of the biggest weddings of the year, and my dress is sleeveless. It didn't take a brain surgeon to know a hairy body was a no-no.

As soon as Glenda comes back in and lifts off the blanket, she gasps. "Honey! What is this? 1973?"

Glenda walks to the counter and mixes up a potion.

"I won't lie, this is going to hurt. I'm going to call in some backup to help me so we can get it done faster."

Two minutes later, there's another worker dressed in white scrubs gawking at my poor decisions.

"We'll start at the bottom and work our way up," Glenda instructs while she pokes around at my upper lip. "At least that's not an issue."

Glenda hands the other woman a pot of goo, and they start lathering it on my shins.

"Mind telling me what's in your wax?" I ask.

"It's not wax. We use a sugaring technique—sugar, lemon juice, water, and a bit of honey from local Greensea bees. We believe in using only all-natural products at Greensea Glam."

At least it's not paraffin. I don't need petroleum to be slathered all over my entire body.

Glenda's helper puts a piece of paper on the goo, and Glenda pulls it off.

"OUCH!" I yell. "Give me a little warning next time."

"Here's your warning: It's going to hurt like hell for the next thirty minutes, so put on your big girl pants."

And she's right. Slather. Press. Rip. Scream. Repeat.

The calming music I heard earlier no longer soothes my nerves because a marching band with too many snare drums pulses over my skin.

When they're just about done and only have my underarms left, Glenda calls Jac in.

"Look, I don't think her skin is going to handle an exfoliation mask very well. It's pretty irritated as it is. Let's just get her a mani and a pedi and call it a day."

"Ohhh! Bummer!" Jac rubs my arm. "Did it hurt?"

Find a fire extinguisher because my body is on fire. Tiny fire ants are swarming and having a Thanksgiving feast on my skin. "Like hell!"

"We heard a couple of yells out there." Jac laughs at my expense.

That was probably when they did the Brazilian. Thank goodness I told them not to worry about my butt and that a landing strip was more than okay with me.

"Darling, you could have made dreadlocks out of all you had going on," says Glenda.

"Thanks, Glenda. Just add it to our bill." Jac winks at Glenda.

I take a deep breath and wrap the towel a little tighter. "Sorry, Jac. I didn't mean to cause so much trouble."

"You did not cause any trouble. Glad we had the spa booked today and could take care of everything." I've never seen Jac this happy. The world could be on fire, and she might laugh it away.

When she got married to Nick, she paced and twiddled her thumbs. She worried about every detail. Now she's the very definition of carefree—like sunshine in human form. I can't imagine anything derailing her mood.

Glenda and her helper finish my underarms and rub a gentle chamomile and coconut oil concoction on my skin.

"Okay, dear, you'll want to use some aloe vera later. I'm sure Barb has some at the house."

"Thank you. I've learned my lesson." As soon as my plane lands at SFO, I'm off to buy a razor.

"You can get changed now." Glenda and her helper leave me alone with my misery.

The lotion works wonders. I'm lighter, like I've shed more than just hair. And honestly, once I get past the sting, it's kind of nice not having all that extra fuzz clinging to me. Clean, smooth, and weirdly freeing. My body's moving effortlessly.

But that's just for a hot second because the searing pain returns after the moisturizer soaks in, and I vow to use a razor religiously so I never get to this point again.

I hobble out of the treatment room with my dignity barely intact to rejoin the girls who look like they've been wrapped in gold leafing compared to my roughed-up skin. They're radiant.

Each of the bridesmaids is wearing a dress of our choosing from Jac's new favorite designer—a hip local Seattle dressmaker. She's come a long way from our thrift store adventures and raiding her brother's closet. But I suppose that's to be expected when you're in love with a rockstar.

My dress is periwinkle blue—my favorite color—with an overlay of flowers that makes me look like I've wandered out of a meadow.

"Pick your favorite colors, girls!" Jac walks to the racks of nail polish.

"All the colors are from Ann's. Made right here on the island." Glenda looks at me while she gives her sales pitch.

Greensea Gull, a subtle light gray. *Dill of a Day*, green, naturally. *It's Better at Bungalow Bay*, shimmering aquamarine. *Low Tide Lilac,* beautiful purple, and a white shimmery *Ferry Dust*.

We all pick our colors and walk over to the chairs. My pedicurist picks up my feet and looks at my toes. I don't have a fungus or anything, but I do like to walk barefoot. Glenda must sense the tech's hesitation and peers at my feet.

She glances up at me and shakes her head. "We're going to need a sander to remove those calluses." Glenda switches spots so she can work on my feet instead of Jac's.

Clearly, I'm the spa problem child.

"Dais, you met Arianna last night, right?" asks Jac.

"Kind of. She dropped us off at the ferry, so I didn't spend much time with her. Is Oliver pretty into her?"

My feet are ticklish and Glenda has a tight grip on them so I don't pull away.

"Seems like she's really into him," says Tippy. "What did you think?"

"To be honest, her energy was all over the place. I couldn't get a good read on her."

As soon as Arianna got out of the car, I noticed her deep purple aura—confused and misused power—but I don't dare share that with them and start any trouble.

"Might have been the concoction you took on the plane," Sylviane reminds me.

"True. And I had my head out the window for most of the drive."

Tippy shakes her head.

"Ollie says she can't wait to meet Johnny! I'm so glad he's met someone who wants to spend time with our family," says Jac.

Glenda brings us each a glass of champagne while warm towels sit wrapped around our legs.

"Ok. I need to know all the plans! Tell me everything about the wedding." Better late than never, I think to myself.

"She has the best wedding planner. You will love Miles, Daisy," says Tippy.

"He is pretty amazing," Jac agrees. "Think *Father of the Bride* goes local. He has created the most divine event with the most Greensea flair ever. We're going to get married on the ferry at sunset under an arch of driftwood and wildflowers. Our signature drink will be a ferry-tini. Everything will be decorated in green, of course. We've hired the local chef, Hunter Sorenson, to make a bang-up farm-to-table meal." Jac takes a breath.

I'm not sure if Jac or the champagne is more bubbly.

Sylviane nods her head and smiles, even though I know she knows the details of the next few days intimately.

"Jac, this is going to be amazing. A true ferry tale," I say.

"That's what I'm selling it as in my columns," claims Tippy.

Sylviane rolls her eyes. "Really, Tip? You've got an angle for everything."

"It's not an angle. Jac and Johnny have granted me exclusive access. I'm only doing what they want me to do."

Good because if Tippy focuses on that, she'll worry less about me kissing Oliver.

Glenda and the crew finish our nails, and we make our way back to the parking lot.

The itching starts as soon as the sea air hits my body. It's a slow build until the burning begins.

"Does your mom have aloe?" I ask Jac.

"I'm not sure, why?" Jac looks at me.

"I'm going to need some to take care of my situation." I circle my hands all over my body.

As soon as Jac pulls up to the house, I sprint out of the car like I'm in the Olympic trials.

My body's on fire. My love life is a mess. And my career is in freefall. But I'm here. With Jac. On Greensea.

And somehow, even through all the stinging, it seems like the start of something good.

CHAPTER FIVE

OLIVER

"For the last time, I don't need help prepping dinner!" Mom waves a spatula around the kitchen.

Mom and Dad—in peak parent mode—insist we go to the bachelor and bachelorette parties with full stomachs even though both Johnny and Jac have promised the goal of the night is not to get rip-roaring drunk.

My brothers, Johnny, and I make a hasty retreat to the deck with beers to bug Dad at his helm, the barbecue.

"Mom kicked us out," I report.

"You boys need to stay out of her happy place." Dad closes the grill and a chorus of laughter announces the girls' return.

"Let's see," says Johnny. Jac shows off her fingernails and sits down on his lap. "Gorgeous."

They kiss, and Josh shields his eyes. "Get a room!" he says and plants a similar kiss on Sylviane's lips.

"Where's Daisy?" asks Dad as a door slams downstairs.

I glance up from my beer just as there's a flash running through the grass, and Daisy stands on the rocks and belly-flops into the bay. My heart leaps into the water with her. Ouch.

Jac, Tippy, and Sylviane exchange a look and crack up laughing.

"What did you three do to her?" My shoulders tense and I'm ready to defend Daisy's honor.

"It wasn't us," says Tippy. "She needed a little more 'work' at Greensea Glam than we thought."

"She's probably trying to cool off the burn," laughs Sylviane.

"Glenda waxed all of her places." Jac makes hand motions covering her entire body. She winks at Mom, who sets a plate of toppings for the burgers on the red and white check tablecloth.

Definitely TMI. "Glad we're all on the same page about oversharing." I, for one, don't need to do any extra thinking about Daisy, and now thanks to them, I am.

"Oh, geez. Was all that necessary for the wedding?" asks Mom, setting the plate on the table.

"Glenda said she hasn't seen that much hair since the 70s," responds Tippy.

"Ok. Ok. Spare us the details," says Dad as he flips a burger.

"Do you have any aloe or anything she can use?" Jac asks Mom.

"Absolutely, sweets. I'll grab my plant for her when she gets out."

I watch Daisy spin as she treads water. Her dark curls splaying across the water like a siren luring me to my doom.

"Ollie, will you bring that poor girl a towel?" asks Dad, giving me a reason to move toward my temptress.

I walk into the laundry room and grab an old striped beach towel and stroll down to the bay. The cool breeze off the water carries the familiar Greensea perfume—part saltwater and part oyster shack. It's only been recently that I've begun to appreciate Greensea again. I was so hellbent on leaving and making my life away from the island, and now I finally appreciate the serenity of the water. The birds. The lapping waves. Maybe it's not only Greensea. Maybe it's the proximity to my family that makes me this way. Maybe it's the someone who believes it's her energy vortex.

"Dais," I yell from the bank. Her head pops up.

"You can't see me like this!" she hisses.

"Like what? I've seen you in a bathing suit a dozen times." I mean how many times have we been right here on the paddleboards over the years? This is nothing new.

The first summer Daisy visited, she had no idea how to paddleboard. She tried and tried, falling over each time, until I got in the water and held the board steady for her. But then she was so excited that she was upright that she jumped off and hugged me. I blamed the cold bay for my shivers that afternoon, but I've always known there was something more that sent my body into overdrive. Her laugh. Her curls. The sparkle in her eyes. But I will it away as usual, and remember Arianna is joining me later tonight.

"No!" she yells. "My skin is burning up, and I look like a bacteria's been feasting on my flesh! And those are only the problems you can see!"

"It can't be that bad." I chuckle. "And even if it is, I don't care."

She doggie-paddles to the beach as I wonder about her other problems and hope they're nothing major.

"Please turn around," she begs.

I do as she asks and hold the towel behind my back, giving her a second to cover up. I turn around slowly and notice red stripes running down her legs, peeking out from under the towel.

"What did Glenda use on you? Sandpaper?"

Daisy blushes on the only part of her that hasn't been manhandled. "No, it's just that there was a lot of hair." She shakes her head. "You don't want to know."

She pulls the towel tighter around her shoulders and we join the others on the deck.

"Sorry about that." Daisy looks at her audience.

"Oh, precious, do not worry for one second," says Mom. "Here's some aloe. Go change, and then we'll have dinner."

Daisy retreats inside with a large leaf from the plant.

"Jac, do you think something else is going on with Daisy?" I ask, taking a sip of my beer.

"What do you mean?" Jac tilts her head to the side.

"I'm not sure, but she doesn't seem like herself and she's made a few comments," I reply. "Just a feeling I have. Seems like it might be more than just that concoction she took on the plane."

"You shouldn't have any feelings about Daisy," says Dave, and I roll my eyes.

"She did mention that work isn't that plentiful. And you know, the wedding and all the social events are not her style," says Jac. "I'll work harder to make sure she's included and comfortable."

"We all will, dear," says Mom. "You focus on the wedding."

Daisy returns looking more like herself in a paisley skirt with fringe on the hem and a long-sleeved white T-shirt. She seems much more relaxed now that her waxing battle scars are hidden. Dad hands her a plate with enough food to feed all of us, Josh pops open a beer for her, and she joins us at the table.

"Hey, Dais," says Jac. "When does Adam get in?"

Daisy picks up her beer and takes a long sip. "Um, oh. Well." She chews on the inside of her lip.

Jac and I exchange looks. I hope mine says, *I told you something was wrong with her.*

"What is it, Dais?" Jac asks.

Daisy picks up her fork and sets it down again. Her shoulders slump forward. "He's not coming."

Sound the alarm. Daisy is dateless.

"What?!" says Jac with a little too much expression.

Daisy balls up her napkin and smashes it onto the table before she takes a deep breath and blurts it out. "He used the ticket you so generously gave him to fly up to Seattle, and then he bought himself another ticket to head to Alaska to see the Northern Lights. The kP index forecasts stronger than normal geomagnetic activity, and he couldn't resist. He says there's a chance he'll make it to the actual wedding if the forecast is correct and he sees them tonight, but I told him not to bother."

What the hell is this guy thinking? I jumped on a plane to fly back and forth to help Daisy, and he can't even be bothered to come to a free wedding?

"Of course he did, because why attend a wedding on your arm when he can chase phantom space lights," I spit out before I notice Daisy looks like a popped balloon. "Shit. Sorry, Dais. Didn't mean to rub your face in it."

Open mouth, insert foot.

"What a wanker!" says Johnny. "The Northern Lights happen all the time, but our wedding is a once-in-a-lifetime event!"

Jac takes Daisy's balled-up napkin and throws it at Johnny. "We're not the point!"

"Oh, yeah. Yeah. Of course, I know that! You're not dating him are you, Daisy?" Johnny attempts a recovery, and I eagerly await her answer, even though it should not matter one iota.

"No, I friend-zoned him a long time ago, but thought he'd be the perfect person to bring to the wedding because he's usually so much fun to have around...I guess that's only true when there's nothing better going on." Her shoulders sit a little easier now that she has that off her chest.

If my entire family weren't sitting around the table, I'd text Arianna and acknowledge the real state of our relationship, offer to be Daisy's date, and promise she'd never be second best.

Sylviane, who's always quiet during our raucous family events, says, "It's his loss, Daisy. Spending time with you is the real treat."

Jac does what I wish I could do and wraps her arms around Daisy.

"I'm sorry, Jac," says Daisy. "I hope this doesn't mess up your numbers and place settings too much."

Typical Daisy, always worrying about her impact on those around her. Last time she stayed here, she used the same plate and silverware the entire time, so she didn't add to the dishwashing load.

Mom stands behind Daisy and squeezes her shoulders. "Do not worry about a thing. Miles will take care of everything. That's what he's here for!"

Daisy takes a bite of her burger and lets out a moan. "This is so good, Tom. How'd you make it?"

I look at her burger. "Shoot! It's ground beef." I reach to take it from her. "Where are the veggie burgers, Dad?"

Mom and Dad exchange a glance. "Oops," says Dad. "Forgot you were a vegan!"

She pushes my hands away and stares at the burger like she wants to take it to bed. Is it normal for a person to be jealous of a piece of meat?

"I don't like to eat anything with a head," Daisy replies. "But, to be honest, I'm more of a fegan lately." Daisy takes a second bite.

"What's that?" Sylviane asks.

"A fake vegan," offers Josh.

"You don't have to be anything around us," says Mom.

"I'm sorry my wedding weekend hasn't been the easiest for you so far. First your mom freaked out about the plane ride. Then Glenda manhandled you. And now Adam isn't coming. Your luck's about to change," says Jac. "I know it!"

"Eat up, people. I don't want any of you to be stumbling drunk after this party," reprimands Dad.

"Dude, when's Arianna coming?" asks Dave.

"Picking her up off the 6:05 ferry from Seattle. She's a fast walker, so I'll leave here around 6:34," I answer.

Dave laughs.

"What's her mile per minute?" asks Josh.

Precision is my thing. I know exactly how long it takes to get from the house to the ferry terminal, maximizing my time so I don't have to wait for Arianna to walk off the boat and can pull up just as she emerges.

"Don't make fun of him," says Mom. "He's been focused on his numbers since he figured out what they

were. And it's proven to be a lucrative career for him."
Mom nods in my direction.

"Better than making maps," I say. While my love is
with numbers, Josh prefers maps—but since jobs are few,
he's had to dress as a party pirate to hawk his treasure
mapmaking skills with the birthday party set.

"Which is better than spending my time with crus-
taceans," Josh says to Dave who owns a shellfish farm and
harvests oysters.

Dad jumps into the conversation. "You're all very
different. Obviously, your mother and I did a bang-up job
raising you to figure out what your interests are. And none
of those interests is better than the others."

A lot of the time, when I'm with my family, it's like
I'm watching a three-ring circus. One of us is attempting
to cross the high wire. Another is throwing flames while
the other two attempt to shoot each other out of a cannon.
The crazier we get, Dad's the jolly clown egging the audience on for more applause. And Mom? She's the ring-
master running around with a fire extinguisher and a net
to catch us. It doesn't matter how old we are; that doesn't
change. Dave and Josh are usually the instigators, ganging
up on me or battling each other.

We're way too old to be reprimanded by our dad, but
old habits die hard, and bickering has always been our
favorite pastime.

"I'm over the moon that you three have dates so I
don't have to worry about you taking advantage of poor
Daisy during a wedding hookup." Jac winks at her.

"Like when you hooked up with Elliott Edwards
when I brought him home during spring break?" Dave
fires at Jac. Her eyes go wide.

I remember that night. I had tried to cover for her and

say Elliott and I were out on the water together, but it figures that Elliott spilled the beans to Dave at some point.

"I, but, I..." Jac stammers.

"That was the end of our friendship. I knew the way Elliott used girls, and there was no way he was going to do that to my little sis," Dave spits out like the transgression happened yesterday.

"Well, at least we know he wasn't the one who got away," says Jac.

"We've all matured. Aren't we old enough to not have to worry about the family rules anymore and just be trusted to act like decent human beings?" asks Josh.

I raise my beer in agreement.

"Never too old for family rules..." mumbles Dad.

"Oh boys, don't forget we wouldn't have needed the rule if you hadn't left your athletic cups in the kitchen or teased little Mara Montgomery so much that she developed a crush that led to sixty-three failed sleepover attempts, countless love notes, and a best friends necklace smashed to smithereens when Dave ignored her."

"Sherman boys—heartbreakers since birth!" Daisy laughs.

I chew slowly, pretending the burger's the reason for my silence and not the fact that Daisy's here, dateless, burning, and the person I most want to sit next to.

GREENSEA GAZETTE

Islanders,

Meet Miles Marryright, wedding planner for the stars. I mean, come on—with that name what else could he possibly be? We're so lucky to have him here. His name's on the byline of every Hollywood wedding you can think of. Ben and Jen (first one)? Check.

I spent the afternoon with him recently. While he's delighted to have a new canvas to work with—Greensea— he is nervous that it may be a little too pedestrian for such a famous wedding. So instead of trying to Hollywood it all up, he's leaning into island lore with a flair. This is going to be an event you'll tell your kids about.

I can confirm that the bachelor and bachelorette parties will take place this evening at The Old Owl. Miles has created a thumping party spot. The deck at The Old Owl is covered by a tent and has been turned into a Latin dance club. Words we never thought we'd utter on Greensea.

Quinn has created The Johnny Nickel—a concoction made from Pimm's and gin—and the Jac Attack—made with vodka, strawberries, and Prosecco. She's also made bite-sized club sandwiches—the Sherman family's favorite—and other apps. Miles thought the bachelor party needed a rhumba lesson. Take it from me: Sherman boys are not natural dancers so this is going to be interesting. Stay tuned for more details tomorrow!

You've all asked and I'll be honest, I don't have the answers about the superyacht that's been lurking near Grays Bay. It looks larger than Thin Pines Country Club. It appeared in the middle of the night this week. By the looks of it, there's a hot tub on the top level towering over three stories. Using my binoculars, I can see there's a dining deck on the second level and a large swim platform on the bottom. If I were the boat, I'd be hanging in Hawaii or the Caribbean but they've picked the emerald waters of our fair island. GG will keep you posted if we get any more information. And as usual, pass on any information if you have it.

Before I sign off, another word from Mayor Nickerbottom. The city council appreciates the fortitude of the continued gnome display and is currently revising ordinances to officially classify nylon inflatable tube gnomes as prohibited structures on Greensea. The city of Greensea will not be broken.

If I were the mayor, I'd give up the fight. Seeing the green and blue inflatables with little red hats waving in the wind was a highlight on my bike ride to Pilates at The Reformation. We're so lucky to have the creative folks who live on our island!

xoxo,

GG

CHAPTER SIX

OLIVER

I plant a kiss on Arianna's cheek as she gets in the car, but she doesn't return the gesture, which is fine since I'm dreaming about kissing someone else.

"You look lovely," I venture.

She yanks the visor down and examines her reflection. "The ferry messes with my hair. No matter where I sit or what I do, the wind gets it. I cannot get used to that."

She pushes her slick-backed bun down.

"Around here, we love to say ferry hair, don't care," I offer.

"Hmmph." Arianna purses her lips, making a duck face. "That's not something I'm interested in."

Wait...is she not interested in riding the ferry or just getting her hair messed up?

Even though I don't live on Greensea, it's a huge part of my life, and the apparent slight on the ferry should sting. But instead, I make a mental note that it's just another reason we're not soulmates.

But tonight's not for disagreements, so I change the subject.

"The party's at The Old Owl—my cousin Quinn's place."

"Is there anything your family doesn't own?" she asks with a sigh.

We're an original Greensea family. Third generation Greensea. My great-grandparents moved to the island from the city when there was only a mosquito fleet of boats running to different destinations on the island. They started the first general store, Cedar & Fern, which is now run by Josh and my parents. My great-grandpa Earl started The Old Owl. My great-uncle Phil founded the *Greensea Gazette*. One of my oldest cousins, Quinn, runs The Old Owl now. The store, the bar, and my family are what's left of Sherman living history.

And the Arianna I knew before today was interested in all things Sherman and Greensea—and me. This Arianna is acting like we're all some kind of punishment.

"Get ready! Miss Kitty and her husband, Kit, are teaching us how to dance tonight!" Even Arianna won't be able to hold that sourpuss face while she's taking dance lessons from Miss Kitty.

"There's someone named Miss Kitty, and she married a Kit?" Arianna squints her eyes and turns up a corner of her mouth.

"Yes! They're Greensea legends. Miss Kitty taught Jac ballet."

Kit's living out his second career as a dance instructor and president of the Miss Kitty Fan Club.

"Of course she did." Arianna applies a new coat of lip gloss. Then wets her fingers and rubs at her flyaway hairs again. "Riding the ferry should be illegal. It's like I've come to a Third World country."

"Hardly think an island community ten miles from Seattle is anything close to Third World."

The Arianna who stepped off the ferry isn't the same girl I met last month. Back then, she was curious about everything—about me. Now she's distant, sharp around the edges. Like the excitement's faded already, and I'm just background noise.

"Anywhere you have to take a boat to get to is not first world." She practically spits her words out.

"Arianna, is there something you want to talk about before we go to the party?"

She flips the mirror up.

"No...but tonight has to be perfect. That's all." Her smile shows off her molars.

At least we can agree on that. "Yes. Perfect for Jac and Johnny."

"Hmmph," she says again as I park my car.

Arianna stays three steps ahead of me as we walk toward the bar. As grumpy as she was in the car, it seems she can't wait to get inside.

Servers dressed in fringed red dresses, greet us at the entrance, holding trays of drinks labeled *The Johnny Nickel* and *Jac Attack*. Sheets of deep red silk line the wood-paneled walls while red light bulbs give off sultry vibes. Heat radiates through the room already filled with bodies. We've been transported to a club somewhere far from Greensea.

In the middle of the entrance is the gigantic heart filled with photos that Mom and Anne have been collaging for days. Think of an elementary school Valentine's Day card filled with doilies, sequins, and baby Jacs and Johnnys. It doesn't match any of the decor, but Mom's vowed to take it to every wedding event all weekend. Miles is doing his best to make it a central focus.

Arianna stops and scans the room. The guys are on one side, and the girls are all huddled together like we're at a middle school dance.

My eyes are immediately drawn to Daisy. She's wearing a long cream skirt and her signature denim vest with bangles up both arms. I can't help but smile at the feather boa wrapped around her neck. Her hair's loose with curls cascading down her back. She twirls a few strands and laughs at something Sylviane says, and my heartbeat quickens. Damn it. Not now.

Arianna chooses *The Johnny Nickel* and beelines toward the guys. Josh offers a wave. Dave lifts his chin in greeting. And Johnny puts out his hand. "Hi, I'm Johnny. You must be Oliver's girlfriend."

Arianna blushes. "I'm his plus one."

My cheeks warm. Yesterday, she got mad when I called her my friend. Maybe this is her revenge.

"I loved your latest album," she gushes, grabbing Johnny's hand. "Your words spoke to my heart."

"Well, when you have a subject like my gorgeous fiancée, it's hard to go wrong," he says.

Arianna coughs. "I'm sure you take inspiration from many sources." She bats her eyelashes like she's trying out for one of his music videos.

I'm about to peel her off of Johnny when someone hits me on the back.

"Oliver Twist! How are you, lad?" Sam, Johnny's bandmate and best friend, wraps me in a hug.

"Ollie!" Johnny's mom, Anne, is right behind him.

"Great to see you!" I turn to Arianna. "Arianna, this is Johnny's mom."

"Of course it is! Anne, so nice to meet you." Arianna smothers her in an embrace like they've known each other for decades.

Thankfully, Miss Kitty and Kit end the awkward interaction when they step onto the deck and clap from the center of the makeshift dance floor, calling everyone to attention.

"Goooood evening, daaaarlings," Miss Kitty purrs. "Are you ready to rrrrhuuuumba?"

A couple of people hoot and holler. Someone whistles.

Johnny solo-rhumbas across the dance floor to more cheers. He doesn't need lessons, and that's good because the Sherman brothers need all of the attention from the teachers. I have two left feet and no sense of rhythm. Even though I'm athletic and an Ironman triathlete, moving to the beat escapes me.

As Johnny reaches the other side of the deck, my eyes turn to Arianna, who's shed her cardigan down to her elbows and is shimmying across the room to meet Johnny. Even the music slows to a crawl; her hips move to a beat that doesn't match the rhythm.

What is she doing?

Tippy raises an eyebrow. Sylviane looks like she's engrossed in a Telenovela. Daisy bites her lip, and Jac's smile freezes in place.

Johnny shoots me a look that screams, *save me*. Instead, our unsung hero, Miss Kitty, breaks the tension once again.

"Ohhh, we have two stars on the dance floor," coos Miss Kitty.

Johnny laughs and moonwalks away from Arianna, making his departure look totally natural.

"Let's make a line. Women on one side and men on the other." Kit and Kitty position us across the deck.

Arianna hustles toward Johnny again, but Miss Kitty —all grace and smiles—slides in and intercepts her, positioning her across from me.

I mouth, *"What are you doing?"*

Arianna shrugs and giggles.

Down the line, Daisy's paired with Sam. Great—she's with another charming rockstar, and I'm with someone who thinks the ferry is Third World.

Sam sways his hips and makes little guns with his hands, and Daisy laughs.

My stomach quivers as I watch them interact. Am I hungry? Were Dad's burgers not cooked all the way?

No, that's not it. I shake my shoulders and try to get a hold of myself. I can't be with Daisy, and she's not alone. Her happiness should make me happy, not open up a crater in my soul.

"Men, take your partner's right hand and hold it with your left. Women place the other hand on their waist," instructs Kit.

Arianna's head toggles from left to right—at least she's staying in one place—but she won't make eye contact with me.

I watch as Sam puts his arm around Daisy—as instructed—and I'm wracked by another pang in my stomach.

Focus, Oliver.

I try to catch Arianna's eyes and wonder what's going on underneath that slicked-back bun.

"Men, you're the leader. Step forward, step right, step left, step back." Miss Kitty demonstrates the move.

"Oh la la," says Kit. "You all look faaaabulous."

"Now, ladies, move to the left and switch partners," meows Miss Kitty.

Arianna moves toward Dave. At least he'll be able to handle whatever she throws at him. I take a deep breath as Mom makes her way toward me.

"Oh, sweetie! All that triathlon training is making you quite the dancer!"

She's trying to make me feel better because I just stepped on her toe.

"Thanks, Mom."

"Arianna has quite a presence," says Mom. She's great at sugarcoating truths. "How's it going with you two?"

If only I could begin to tell her that I don't imagine Arianna lasting beyond the weekend.

"It's fine," I say and focus on the music.

"And right, and left." The cues continue in the background.

"Switch," says Kit, tapping his foot to the beat.

Jac's my next dance partner. She's grinning from ear to ear. Her cheeks are going to ache when this weekend's done.

"Oi! Isn't this so much fun?"

"Sure is, sis," I deadpan.

"And then switch again!" says Kit.

This time, Daisy makes her way to me.

"Feeling better?" I ask, hoping the spa visit didn't have many lingering effects.

"It's not as bad as the time I was pelted with sand at Burning Man, but after another Jac Attack, I don't think I'll feel anything anyway."

I place my hand on her waist, my thumb slipping under her vest. Her bangles jingle when I take her hand. Her smile reaches the corners of her twinkling blue eyes. Her skin's still warm as it melts into me like butter. I shouldn't notice this. I shouldn't care. But everything in me does. Even my shoulders relax as I breathe in the familiar intoxicating scent of Daisy—part earth, part vanilla frosting, part wild child.

I don't know what it is about her—we're opposites in most ways—but she's an elixir for my soul.

Visions of the albino deer kiss flood my head and I'm caught in the memory of her soft lips and her tongue. Every part of me wishes I could plant my lips on hers right now, right here, in the middle of the dance floor.

Kit purrs cues in the background, and I close my eyes and focus on the music, or at least enjoy this moment and imagine a time where Daisy and I could be together.

Miss Kitty walks up behind me and whispers, "Oh la la," into my ear. My cheeks turn the color of Miss Kitty's dress, pulling me out of my reverie, and I drag my hands away from Daisy before anyone else notices.

"I'm thirsty. Are you thirsty?" I ask like a nervous seventh grader at his first dance.

One wrong step and I'll taint the whole wedding weekend for Jac. For Johnny. For everyone. I can't do that. No matter how right this seems, it's not my moment.

"Sure!" answers Daisy. "Let's take a break."

I place my hand on the small of her back, leading her to the bar.

She takes a step back. "I'm going to sneak off to the ladies' room." She half smiles and slips away.

Is she upset? Are we on the same wavelength? Or is

she trying to get away from me? Maybe she heard Miss Kitty.

My mind spirals, and I look up at the owl, even the bar's mascot is wearing a veil. And I swear that piece of taxidermy winks at me.

Shit. I am out of control.

I prop my head up on the bar and switch my focus to my other issue. Arianna's heading toward Johnny and Sam. Lurking behind them like a creeper with her oversized purse. She's starstruck in the worst way. Sam turns around and nods at her, then turns back to the circle, not letting her in. Like a babysitter watching his charge, I mosey over to them and ask if she wants anything to drink.

"Beer? Gin and tonic?" I ask trying to break her from her Johnny induced trance.

"Um. Yeah. A beer would be good," she says without looking at me. I don't want her to pay attention to me, but I don't want her to stalk my almost brother-in-law either.

Tippy and Sylviane are huddled together at the bar.

"Are you two up to no good?" I ask.

Tippy stares at Arianna. "I don't think we could drag your date away from Johnny if we tried, Ol."

Yeah, she's right. Johnny must get that all the time, though.

"How'd you two meet?" asks Sylviane.

"At a work event a month ago. She works for one of my clients."

She was really into me when we first met. She knew everything about me. I was impressed by how forward she was, walking right up to me to introduce herself.

"We bonded over running. She asked me to help her come up with a training plan for an upcoming race."

We still haven't run together, but I did give her a detailed plan based on the running speeds and goals she shared with me.

Tippy and Sylviane exchange a look.

"What?" I ask.

"Oh, nothing," says Sylviane, and they walk toward the bathroom like co-conspirators.

And I return to my plus one, counting the minutes until this night is over.

CHAPTER SEVEN

DAISY

The guitar strums float in like fog under the bathroom door while I lean into the cold metal stall, still trying to cool the part of me Ollie's hand just lit on fire. His touch —ugh, it's still echoing on my back like a secret tattoo. And now I'm hiding in here because how am I supposed to waltz back out there and pretend nothing happened— to Jac, to the whole shiny, perfect Sherman crew—when everything inside me is like a piñata ready to explode?

The bathroom door swings open, bringing sounds of laughter and clinking glasses, and two more sets of footsteps.

"She's not here for Oliver," whispers a voice that sounds like Tippy.

"I agree," says Sylviane, most likely.

I peek through the crack in the stall to get a better view. Yep. Tippy, with her arms crossed, with a finger tapping her chin. And Sylviane tilting slightly as she leans against the sink.

Tippy's head turns in my direction, and before I can move, her eyes peer in at me.

"What are you doing in there?" she asks.

"Catching my breath and clearing my aura," I say instead of *dreaming about a forbidden boy*.

"Come out here," she commands and continues talking to Sylviane, "She's not at all interested in Oliver. Instead, she's fawning over Johnny."

"Yeah, what was that almost striptease she did across the dance floor?" I ask.

"Suddenly Oliver's chopped liver!" Sylviane proclaims and then hiccups. "Oops! That was me. Blame the Jac Attack—and the three before it. She's more concerned about her slicked-back bun than she is Oliver."

The bathroom door swishes open again, this time bringing Arianna clutching her purse to her chest, looking like she just swallowed a canary. Or at least has one in her oversized bag.

The three of us exchange a look.

"What do you have in there?" Tippy asks.

"Nothing. Just, um, my hair products. Arianna doesn't move out of the doorway.

"I've been meaning to ask what kind you use. Your hair is so shiny." Sylviane seems so innocent while she asks leading questions.

"I do keratin treatments," Arianna replies.

And then with a smack of the door, Arianna stumbles and lets go of her bag, causing it to fly out of her arms as Miss Kitty walks into the bathroom. A beer bottle shatters on the floor. A pile of scrunched-up custom *Johnny + Jac* napkins with Jac's name ripped off land on the sink. A cocktail fork clinks on the tiles. And a dozen pictures of

Johnny as a baby, toddler, and teenager drop like confetti to the ground.

"I'm sorry, daaarrrling," Miss Kitty meows.

"What the hell?" Sylviane asks as Arianna bends down and tries to shove all of the contents back into her bag.

"Are you collecting these things to place on an altar in your apartment or selling them on eBay?" Tippy asks Arianna as she crawls around the floor.

Arianna scrunches her face and ekes out, "Both?"

"No one move." Tippy turns to me. "I'm getting Sam." And she disappears, leaving us with the perpetrator.

Miss Kitty looks Arianna up and down. "With the rigid moves of your hips, I knew you weren't a Rhumba Queen."

Miss Kitty is bringing the heat.

For the fourth time, the bathroom door opens, revealing Tippy and Sam.

"We've seen this before." Sam stands with his hands on his hips.

"You have other people who collect your garbage?" Sylviane hiccups again.

"People take everything from us. We've had hotel maids steal our pillowcases and our towels. Dirty underwear. Sweat socks. You name it, people want it. A lot of times the things pop up on an online auction site."

He takes a step closer. "Johnny didn't want security at these little gatherings. We've only arranged it for the wedding because there will be so many people there. You know how he feels about Greensea—he trusts everyone on the island. The wedding seemed smart because it would be a large group of people out at sea."

"Arianna is not from Greensea," Sylviane blurts out. "The rest of the island is safe."

"How much would these things go for?" I look at the bag of garbage and wonder if there's really a market for this kind of thing.

"Not now, Burning Girl," says Tippy.

Sam makes a phone call, and two minutes later, a burly man walks into the bathroom.

"You take it from here," says Sam to the guy.

"I thought you said Johnny didn't want security?" I ask.

"He didn't, but as I was about to say, I'm not stupid enough to not have it running in the background." Sam taps on his phone. "The lawyers are on it and will send over a cease and desist. We won't have to worry about her again."

The guard walks Arianna out of the bathroom, and we follow like ducklings.

Sam pulls Oliver aside and whispers. I'm not good at reading lips, but my best guess is that he said, "What the hell?"

Holy chakras! He must be so mad and embarrassed. I mean, his date was stealing garbage and not because she was hungry. It's taking every ounce of my willpower not to run to his side and whisper sweet mantras in his ear.

He runs his hands through his hair. Then looks at his watch like it has all the answers. His perfectly pressed shirt is buttoned up as tightly as his mood.

When Arianna reaches the door, she turns to Ollie and says, "You're not so bad on the eyes either, Oliver. You might have a future on OnlyFans."

Oliver shakes his head and opens his mouth, but nothing comes out.

"I'll get her on the next ferry, Mr. Sherman," says the security guard as he walks her out the door.

She didn't just get exiled: she made an exit to remember.

As horrified by the situation as I should be, I have to admit there's a part of me that's thrilled Ollie's date is walking the plank.

In an attempt to eat my feelings, I grab a mini club sandwich—momentarily abandoning my vegan guilt, again—and stuff it in my mouth just as Ollie walks over to me.

"I can't believe I was dumb enough to be played by her."

My mouth's full and I try to chew the club roll as fast as I can. But I stand there and nod, letting my eyes do the talking.

After I finish chewing the sandwich like it was my last meal, I put my hand on his arm. "I'm sorry, Ol. She's shifty and took advantage of your kindness."

Oliver smiles softly. Our eyes catch like a magnet looking for its pole, only separating when Sylviane and Josh walk over and hand us each a beer.

"Cheers," says Josh. "You could do better anyway."

"Let's do Jac and Johnny a favor and not let them know," says Oliver. "Pretend she got sick and didn't want to contaminate the rest of us. They don't need my love life adding to the drama of the weekend."

Kit strays from the theme of the night and cues up a country tune while Miss Kitty claps her hands.

"Time for some line dancing, my kittens," she says.

A few yee-haws ring out from the crowd, and Oliver and I get in line. We sidestep as a cowboy croons about an achy breaky heart. Each time we clap and touch our hips, the air around us sizzles.

Oliver grabs my hand and gives me a twirl; we're freeforming our line dancing. Our eyes meet, and I swear he grips my fingers tighter. We twirl to the other side, and my giddy mood jumps as I close my eyes and listen to the music. I'm like a toddler twirling around in her first long skirt. I put a little more oomph into my next twirl, but as I do it, the right side of my skirt catches the anklet on my left foot, pulling my foot the other way, and I end up in a heap in the middle of the floor.

"Daisy!" yells Ollie, rushing to my side. He's practically on top of me, lifting me from my waist. His long fingers find their way under my vest. I know it's not intentional, but a girl can dream.

He sets me on my feet and offers me a hand as I straighten myself out.

"Are you okay?"

My skirt is hopelessly tangled around my anklet, and the more I try to free it, the worse I make it. I might as well be wrapped in a fishing net. Ollie notices I'm still tied up, crouches down, and gives it a shot. His efforts don't fare much better—I'm officially equal parts helpless and ridiculous. He's right there, focused and gentle. I try to think about anything other than how close his face is to my thigh.

"I'm fine. Just a little embarrassed." I finally eek out.

Ollie stands up and grabs a chair. "This is going to take a little more work than I thought."

Jac wraps her arms around my neck. "Sweetie! Are you okay?"

She's giggly and maybe a little tipsy. She deserves to be at her party.

"Grab some scissors from Miss Kitty," says Oliver.

Johnny goes instead and comes back a minute later. All I can do is stare at Oliver sitting at my feet, untangling me. He's so gentle and careful and I can't remember the last time a man attended to my needs like this. I must be all googly-eyed because Tippy comes up behind me and whispers, "Snap out of it!"

My cheeks turn red, and I look away as Oliver cuts the anklet from my skirt.

"Thanks," I mumble as the DJ yells last song. Oliver offers me his hand, presumably to dance. "I think I'll sit this one out."

If I keep dancing with him, I might fall again—and not just on the floor.

GREENSEA GAZETTE

Islanders,

Oh did we ever move our hips to the beat at the party last night! Pop stars are born to rhumba. The rest of us are just human and woke up a little bit sore. It was steamy and dreamy and set the tone for the wedding weekend.

Security is tight on Greensea Island. Even after the latest infiltration by a guest who tried her darndest to get into the inner circle (thwarted by none other than me), we're asking you to help keep the wedding guests safe and report anything unusual you might see. Keep an eye out on the ferry and feel free to ask anyone any questions. We're all in this together, islanders.

The legend of the Greensea Sea Goon lives on. Daryl Hattentale claims to have seen it on the late 4:45 ferry on Tuesday night. It raised a fin and he swears he heard a bark. The image he captured on his phone appears to be a gigantic elephant seal, although larger than any that's been recorded. I, for one, am not taking any chances and will not be going out on a paddleboard anytime soon.

The island's all abuzz about our new ferry captain—aptly nicknamed Ferry McSwoony. His crisp white uniform stretches across an ample chest, and he towers over the steering wheel as he guides the boat into Grays Bay. The Washington State Department of Transportation would like to tell his adoring fans that Captain Ferry McSwoony will not be attending to medical emergencies on the boat. Translation: Stop fake fainting. His luscious lips and impressively large hands are not going to administer CPR.

xoxo,

GG

CHAPTER EIGHT

OLIVER

Sneaking out of the house for a run, I try not to wake anyone after our big night. The steady rhythm of my feet hitting the ground usually lulls me into calm. I'm hoping today's no different.

The early morning dew hangs on the trees as I whip through the cobwebs on the trail. Temperatures in July are still cool enough to get a decent run in. I can't imagine living in a climate other than this. The PNW may be dark all winter, but our reward is the beautiful summer days.

All my muscle memory kicks in when I run these trails. I'm faster here than in the concrete jungle across the sound. Over the hill. Down the trail. By the pontoon boat overgrown with moss and ferns, covering up the lost dreams of Crandall Wharton and his Greensea Safari business. Farmstands filled with fresh eggs in a rainbow of colors. Mason jars filled with daisies—reminding me of the real-life Daisy who's a breath of fresh air whenever I see her.

I try to picture what it would look like—saying it out loud, laying it all on the table. But the risk is gargantuan—like waiting for a ferry without looking at the schedule. In her mind, I'm nothing more than her best friend's dependable brother. What if I'm not the cheese on her veggie burger, but just the side of organic potato salad she tolerates?

I can't wreck this. Can't blow up whatever fragile friendship exists between us with my inconvenient feelings. Losing her completely—not being in her orbit, not hearing her bangles jingle down the hallway or watching her light up when she talks about moon tea or Joshua Tree —that wouldn't be worth it.

So I'll stay right here. Be the best best friend's brother. Quietly orbiting, always near, never quite close enough. Because if I can't have her the way I want, I'll take her any way I can.

I smell the tide before I get to Bungalow Bay. Musky, briny, damp oysters. Some people hate it, but a true Greensea-er loves it.

Dave and his bright yellow waders trudge through the water. I pick out the perfect skipping stone and sail it out across the bay to Dave with precise leaps.

"What the hell, man?" He jumps and pulls off his headphones.

"Do you sleep out there?"

I stop my watch and sit on one of Sherman Shellfish's picnic tables while he marches back in with his oysters. He and Tippy have done a lot with this place. They made it into a little destination for roadside snacks. Even if the irregularity of being self-employed makes me nervous, I can appreciate what he's doing from afar.

"You're up early," Dave says as he plunks down a bucket.

I nod. It's hard to sleep when I'm pining for someone a few bedrooms away.

"Did you hear from Arianna after she got voted off the island?" Dave asks.

"No, and I blocked her number."

Dave shakes his head. "Still can't believe people do things like that."

"Me either."

I couldn't sleep last night, so I spent some time on some auction sites. There's no doubt that people make money off that crap. I saw a listing for Mick Jagger's straw for $500. These people have more than one screw loose.

"You seem to be handling the 'breakup' well." He uses air quotes.

I shrug. "We weren't dating for that long, and I had some misgivings before Garbage-gate anyway." Like her name was Arianna and not Daisy.

"Do you think she found you organically, realized your connection to Johnny, and then saw an opportunity to monetize her crush? Or do you think she had a crush on Johnny and tried to find a way in?"

"Good question. I didn't think anything of it when she introduced herself at the work party, but our Sherman family picture—you know that selfie Mom took of all of us last year on the beach—has been in every tabloid. It wouldn't be hard to find any of us."

"You dodged a bullet." Dave dumps a bunch of shells into a bucket. "Harvesting for the wedding."

"A lot of pressure."

"Nah, like you said, I do this in my sleep."

"Later, bro," I say and restart my watch and begin the

climb up the hill toward home. Past the milk truck. Around the Spoke Dads—a dozen middle-aged guys on road bikes.

The forest is still quiet, and I nearly fling myself off the trail when a figure suddenly emerges from the tall grass. It takes me a moment to realize it's Daisy standing in front of me, dressed in overalls and a tank with a purple bandana holding her hair back.

"You almost gave me a heart attack!" I yell.

She pulls her earbuds out. "Sorry! I didn't hear you coming."

My watch lets out a little alarm letting me know my heart rate is too high. I bend over and put my hands on my knees, trying to bring it down.

"Are you okay?" Daisy asks.

"Yeah, I need to catch my breath."

Daisy rubs my back. My heart rate alarm dings again. Shit. There's no denying the way my body feels about her. Every part of me wants to roll around in the grass with her. I should remove my watch before it gives me away.

I take a deep breath and stand up.

"Walk back?" I ask.

"Sure!"

"What are you doing out here so early?"

"Couldn't sleep, so I went for a walk. I'm listening to this great podcast about the healing powers of mushrooms, so I dipped off the trail to look for some." She sticks her hand in the pocket of her overalls and pulls out a dozen assorted fungi. "Look at all the mushrooms that are hiding right in front of us."

"Are those poisonous?" I ask while I try to recall all my mushroom identification lessons from Boy Scouts.

"Poisonous?" She drops them on the ground like they've caught fire.

"Yes, you can't just eat any mushroom. You need to be trained in identifying them. You're not a forest gnome."

Daisy looks at her hand. "Relax. I only licked one."

"Daisy!" My heart rate alarm dings again.

"Chill, I'm just kidding. I didn't...I don't think." She winks at me.

She wipes the evidence of her fungi hunt on her overalls before we walk down the driveway.

Her phone pings, and she looks at it and then shoves it in her pocket.

"Everything ok?"

"Just real life trying to kill my joy!" She skips down the path and toward the house, then turns and yells, "Thanks for saving me from the deadly fungi! You'll always be my knight in shining armor, Ollie."

I stop and try to restore my heart to its resting rate. Man, she revs me up...in all the ways.

CHAPTER NINE

DAISY

The Sherman deck is a temporary refuge for the wedding party as we enjoy a moment of quiet before the next nuptial activity begins.

The sun's out with rays dancing across the bay. I love how the water always looks green here. Like the color of melted sea glass. I never understood why until Jac explained it was the phytoplankton in the water—thankfully different than how Chicago dyes the river for St. Patrick's Day. I could sit on the Shermans' deck forever watching nature. The birds are chirping and I let out a little yelp when an eagle swoops down in front of me, followed by a squawking crow.

Sylviane winks at me. "A symbol of rebirth," she says. "Everything's changing for you."

Good. I need it to change so my landlord stops sending me threatening texts. I make a mental note to look up squatters' rights later.

"Goooood afternoon!" Miles walks out on the deck

and claps his hands together. "How are all of you after that raucous party last night?"

"That was a blast," says Jac. "Thank you, Miles." She hugs him.

"Ol, is Arianna feeling better?"

The group stiffens. Eyes shift from one person to the next. Luckily, Jac was so caught up in her bliss she missed the whole saga.

"Not really," Oliver says. "She won't be joining us."

I tuck my tiny moment of glee away. Having to hide jealousy along with desire would not be my strong suit. Thank you, Universe, for sparing me that.

Jac narrows her eyes. "Why? What happened?"

"Nothing to worry about," Tippy says, swooping in like the pro she is. "We just realized she wasn't here for the right reasons."

As if on cue, a boat honks in the bay, and a ginormous yacht—bigger than the house—makes its way into the cove at the perfect moment.

"That's the boat everyone's been asking me about on GG," says Tippy already yanking her phone out of her pocket and taking a picture. "Who is it and what's it doing here?"

A horn toots again and someone waves from the deck.

"Is that Sam?" asks Johnny. "He always makes a top-dollar entrance."

We watch as the yacht anchors and Sam paddle-boards off the swim platform to the Sherman's beachfront like it's the easiest thing in the world.

"Cheers, mates! Like my new ride?"

"Sam! Why do you have a yacht?" asks Jac.

"Needed somewhere to stay near Greensea if all my best mates are over here."

"Right on," says Johnny, giving him a high five.

Jeez. Maybe Sam will let me stay on the yacht—live in the laundry room and wash all his sheets—until I can figure out my rent situation.

"Okay. Okay. Enough with the fancy arrivals. This weekend is about the bride and groom no matter what you pull up in." Miles glares at Sam who nods back and mouths, "*Sorry.*"

"Let's get busy! I've prepared an amazing island scavenger hunt for all of you!" Miles is bouncing up and down on his tip toes. "We're going to divide you up into teams and give you a list of things you need to find on the island. Everything represents the darling couple and this charming destination."

"Is this going to be too hard for us newcomers?" asks Sam in his sexy British accent.

"Of course not! We have islanders paired with newcomers," replies Jac.

Not being a newcomer or an islander leaves me up for grabs.

"Ok," says Jac. "The teams are as follows: Mom and Anne, me and Dad."

The group lets out a collective "awww."

Jac continues, "Josh and Tippy, Sylviane and Dave, Sam and Johnny, and Daisy and Oliver."

Me and Ollie. I glance his way and flash a double thumbs-up. He's cool as a cucumber with his arms folded across his chest while my insides are fizzing. I'm playing with fire, spending all this time alone with him —but it's Jac who keeps tossing us together like some oblivious matchmaker. Little does she know I'm basically a shaken bottle of kombucha, ready to pop at the mere thought of more time with him. One day I'll tell her how she contributed to her best friend's downfall. But not today.

Jac hands us each a piece of paper. "Here's what you each need to find."

"No fair, Jac. Did you create this?" asks Dave.

"No, Miles did it all. This is my first time seeing it, too."

Miles continues with the directions while Jac finishes handing out the papers. "The most important thing you must do is record every task you complete. I'll be compiling them into a video and we'll share it at the rehearsal dinner. Any questions?" Miles asks.

"How much time do we have?" Josh asks.

"The rest of the day." Miles looks around the room at each of us. "Any other questions?"

"How do we win?" asks Tippy.

"Winning will be two-fold. You will receive points for how quickly you complete all the tasks, and then your answers will be ranked for originality," Miles explains.

"What do we win?" asks Sam.

Miles slaps his own cheeks. "How could I forget? The winning team will walk away with $500 in cash—and the bride and groom will name one of the signature cocktails in your honor!"

Cash? We have to win. $250 won't pay my rent, but it will take the edge off.

"Oh! You can call it the Daisy Fizz!" I smile.

"You have to win first," Miles reprimands me.

I ball up my fists and look at Ollie. He's a natural competitor with all his races and the perfect companion to help me—I mean us—win.

"One more thing!" Miles points to the sky. "If the

Greensea Island police become involved, you're automatically disqualified."

We all nod in acknowledgment.

"Okay. On your marks, get set, and go!" Miles claps us off.

We all break up into our pairs. Ollie and I sit in the armchairs in the family room and study the paper. I tuck my knees under me and read the list.

1. Sing a line from one of Johnny's songs and record it—and yes, it's karaoke-style!
2. Find something old, something borrowed, and something blue—bonus points if it relates to the bride or groom!
3. Take a picture with a wild Greensea animal. Bonus points if it's the llama that bit Sam in the ass.
4. Ask an islander for their best piece of marriage advice and record it.
5. Look for a Greensea landmark that reminds you of the couple. Snap a picture with it.
6. Reenact something from the bride and groom's story as you imagine it happened and video it.

Crap, that's a lot of things to accomplish in an afternoon. Ollie gets up and returns with a pad of paper and a pen.

He scribbles on the paper and looks up. "Ok. If we allocate twenty-five minutes for each task and fifteen minutes to get to and from each spot, we should finish at the top of the heap. Do you have a timer on your phone?"

I crinkle my nose. "Have you met me? You know I don't use a timer. Let's start with the first thing on the list and just wing it." I look over the paper.

"Have you met me?" Oliver counters with a wink.

We're going to have to use our different work styles to our advantage. He's ready to plan a NASA space mission and I'm ready to freewheel it on spring break in Cancun.

"Let's make a deal, Mr. Accountant. I'll agree to watch the time if you agree to unbutton a little. Like we may even complete task six before task five. Let's try to value joy more than hustle."

Ollie rolls his eyes. "I can handle whatever you throw at me as long as it's not poisonous."

"Haha."

The first item's an easy one to tick off.

"Obviously, we need to complete a task at the ferry. That's the most Greensea thing there is." I twirl a lock of hair on my finger. "Want to go sing Greensea Gal down at the terminal? We could complete tasks one and five at the same time!"

"Now you're thinking like a competitor." Ollie nudges my shoulder. "I knew you had it in you!"

We grab our things and run toward Ollie's Tesla. The driveway's empty, meaning we're off to a slow start. Sam and Johnny went toward the yacht, which has to be a slower mode of transportation than the car.

The interior of the car is just like him—neat and tidy, not even a stray straw wrapper to be found.

"You're going to drive and not just program that thing, right?" I ask.

He turns to me with a lopsided look, like I may have

lost my mind. "I thought you knew me better than that. This isn't the self-driving kind. I'd never be able to give up that kind of control."

True. Oliver is the king of managing every little detail.

"Good, because I had a terrible experience in a self-driving Waymo in the city."

"You'd get into a car without a driver, but you wouldn't fly here on your own?"

Touché, but my mom has not presented me with any premonitions about cars yet. "I contain multitudes."

Ollie hmphs to himself. "So what happened in the car?"

"It took me to the wrong address, and I couldn't get it to correct itself. And then the door wouldn't open. I thought I was trapped. A minor panic attack ensued as I banged on the window until a kind stranger explained how to get out of the car from the other side of the window."

"I thought stories like that were urban legends."

"Nope. It happened." I have a magnetic force field that attracts strange occurrences.

Ollie laughs and starts the car.

Making him smile is sunshine for my soul. The flick of his eyelashes, the pop of his dimple—my insides can't handle much more.

And our day together is just beginning.

GREENSEA GAZETTE

Islanders,

Beware! The Sherman Family and their closest inner circle are on a pre-wedding scavenger hunt today! You may be asked to help them complete a quirky task—say yes and be creative! I don't want to give anything away and give any of the teams an unfair advantage, but be on your toes if you see a Sherman out and about! We'll be compiling it all into a video that we'll be sure to share with you. Please do not help anyone cheat, though. The hunt must be completed fair and square.

Kudos to the person or people who decorated the roundabouts with the menagerie of painted driftwood gnomes. What a lovely festive touch! And a way to prolong the silent gnome protest! The figures with a bow tie and a veil—brilliant! I've been asked to tell you that City Ordinance 15.4.1 prohibits these displays as they impede the sightline of oncoming traffic. Blah, blah, blah. Wouldn't you know there's an ordinance for everything, and if there isn't—give it a hot minute and there will be. Has the city considered the impact its landscaping has on incoming traffic? Or the placement of the signs saying no signs or art installations are allowed? Another island head scratcher. The city has said no to plastic, inflatable, and now all-natural wood displays...what will the creatives on Greensea come up with next?

In breaking news, the superyacht belongs to Sam, Johnny Nickel's best mate. He'll be officiating at the wedding and then plans to tour the northern islands in the Puget Sound. Ahoy, matey!

Finally, to address your concern (there was only one—and I have my suspicions), calling our new ferry captain "Ferry McSwoony" is not objectifying a maritime employee. We at the Greensea Gazette, value the new captain for his beliefs, feelings, and yes, his physique. For the record, he graduated summa cum laude from Stanford with a degree in engineering with a concentration in maritime science. Hot and smart. We hear he'll be at the helm on the weekday shift beginning with the 7:05. Wink. Wink. And captaining the MV Tokitae on the wedding day.

xoxo,

GG

CHAPTER TEN

DAISY

At the ferry terminal, we find a spot in the parking lot that's right along the water where the trees part, giving us a perfect vantage point of incoming ferries and the Space Needle in the background.

"I'll record you singing," says Ollie.

I cue up "Greensea Gal" on my phone, roll my shoulders, and prepare to unleash my inner pop star in front of the ferry terminal. Giving it all my energy, I form my hands into a fake microphone and put everything I have into it—moving my hips around, yelling more than singing the tune.

> Your eyes the color of the sea
> Your heart gentle and free
> I live for the love of my Greensea Gal...

Oliver laughs as he records it. "You nailed it, Dais!"

He plays the video back for me and I jump and hold

onto his arm. Maybe I have a career in busking if the graphic design gig doesn't work out.

"Will you look at that?" He shows me his watch. "We got this task done in thirteen minutes and thirty-seven seconds. There's no way the other teams are as fast!"

"Dude, remember you're going to chill on the stopwatch duties? No pacing each task."

He shakes his head, and we walk back to the car. I buckle my seatbelt and read task number two.

Find something blue, something borrowed, and something old—bonus points if it relates to the bride or groom!

"Any thrift stores or places that will barter with us?" I ask and scoot around in the car seat so I'm facing him.

"Hmm...thrift stores might be too obvious. Let's go somewhere more original," says Oliver as he drums on the steering wheel for a minute. "Oh! Got it! Old Man Johnson's barn is filled with treasures he finds at estate sales. I bet Mrs. Johnson would be happy to let us borrow anything."

"Great! I've never been to the farm."

Oliver starts the car.

"The Johnsons' grandson, Thayer, was a friend of mine when we were younger. I played manhunt and other games over there when I was in junior high, but I haven't been back since."

A familiar pang of jealousy stirs in me whenever I think about other people's so-called normal childhoods. Being one of the rare kids who spent their early years at Burning Man and every other festival my parents chased,

I never had a gaggle of kids to play with. I never lacked attention—far from it. But it didn't come from other kids. I was more like a curiosity, a plaything passed around a fire pit, adored by grownups but always on the outside looking in.

We wind along the country road. Ollie sets the cruise control to 17.5 miles per hour to make sure we obey the speed limit and don't draw the attention of the police.

The driveway to the farm is lined with a brown wooden fence and a dozen cows.

"Oh no!" I yell and Ollie slams on the brakes.

"Dais! You can't yell like that when I'm driving. What's wrong?"

"Look! The cows are lying down!" I point to the meadow and the cows lazing about chomping on grass.

"So what? They're tired."

"When a cow lies down, it means it's going to rain."

"We're in Seattle. It always rains." Ollie picks up his phone.

"But rain is less than ideal for an outdoor wedding," I remind him.

"The ceremony is on the top sundeck of the ferry. I'm sure Miles has accounted for every possibility."

He looks something up on his phone and faces it toward me.

"Look. Rain on your wedding day is good luck. It's a sign of a fresh and strong start."

I shake my head. I'm not sure Jac will think that way when her mascara's running down her face.

"And the forecast doesn't have any rain in it." He shows me a graphic with the seven-day outlook.

I shake my head like a doomsday prophet. "The cows

know, Ollie. They sense it in their bones—dip in pressure, rain on the way."

Everything in my life seems to get rained on lately, so this tracks. I hope I'm not the one bringing all the bad luck.

Ollie continues down the drive and parks the car in front of a white farmhouse that looks like it's been plucked from a bygone era. Old Man Johnson's place sits proudly behind a broad gray porch, where hanging ferns sway gently and weathered rocking chairs creak ever so slightly in the breeze, as if waiting for stories to be told. It's like we've stepped back in time. Before we even reach the top step, the screen door swings open with a familiar squeak.

"Hello, Oliver," says Mr. Johnson, dressed in his overalls and straw hat like he walked out of the fields in the early 1900s. "What can I do you for?"

"We have a rather odd request," says Oliver. "My friend Daisy and I are a team for a family scavenger hunt. We're looking to borrow something old and blue. Any chance you have anything?"

Mr. Johnson thinks for a second before he speaks. "I'm sure Mrs. Johnson and I can dig something up for you. Meet me at the barn and we'll see what's out there."

Ollie and I trudge through too-tall grass to a barn that's seen better days. The roof is equipped with several holes and it looks like a woodpecker took out a whole side.

Mr. and Mrs. Johnson practically run to meet us there. Mrs. Johnson is dressed in matching overalls and has a little red bandana tied around her neck. Her yellow aura and good-natured energy pours out of her.

"Oh, Oliver! Introduce me to your lovely date," says

Mrs. Johnson.

"No, no. She's not my date." Oliver holds up his hands like he's trying to stop traffic. "We've just been randomly thrown together for this adventure."

Overkill. I think they get it.

Mrs. Johnson giggles. "Well, anyway...thank you for thinking of us to help you with this hunt! I'm sure we can find something perfect!"

Mr. Johnson slides the barn doors open and my nose is hit with a waft of hay. The barn is gigantic. Half garage, half stall.

"Whoa!" I say looking all around. It's like a vintage market filled with trinkets. Some are even hanging on the wall.

"Yes, there's a lot of stuff out here." Mrs. Johnson pulls her hair back with her bandana.

Ollie drums his fingers against his leg, his eyes darting around the cluttered chaos of the barn. I can practically see the disarray gnawing at his neatly ordered soul.

There's something large covered by a piece of canvas in the back of the barn that piques my curiosity. "What's that?" I ask.

"Oh, just our grandson's faded dreams," says Mrs. Johnson, waving my question off.

"Forgot about Thayer's idea to drive cross country in the bus," says Ollie.

"It's a bus?" I ask.

"Yes, an old VW that Thayer bought back in college. But he fell in love with a girl from Boston and never came back for it," says Mr. Johnson.

"Does it work?" The giddiness is taking over my body.

"It does. Had it down for an oil change at Maggie's garage not too long ago." Mr. Johnson shrugs.

A VW bus is what all my dreams are made of. I used to drool over them as a child, and in recent years, my eyes have been jealous of everyone I've seen around San Francisco. But they're such an out-of-reach item for someone already living outside her means.

"Would you mind if I took a look at it?"

"We're on a tight schedule," Ollie reminds me and I shoot him a look. Schedules and dreams rarely make good travel companions.

Mr. Johnson walks toward it and pulls the canvas off. Underneath sits an immaculate blue VW bus that looks like we just dug it out of a time capsule. I walk around the whole thing slowly. I wipe my mouth as I'm afraid I might be drooling.

"She's perfect."

Ollie and the Johnsons exchange a look.

"And she's blue!" Mr. Johnson winks at me. "Fits the bill for the scavenger hunt item."

"And Johnny rented a VW van when he was on the island for the first time! We'll even get extra points if we use this." My anklet jingles as I bounce in place. "Plus, Jac would just die if we pulled up in something like this!"

"What would we do with my Tesla? There's got to be something smaller that will work."

Ollie walks around inspecting the other treasures.

I pretend I don't hear him, open the door, and sit in the driver's seat. The vinyl's torn a little, but it's like she's made for me. My butt and my legs fit in the seat perfectly. My legs even each the pedals without any adjustments. I peer out the window, employing my biggest puppy-dog eyes. "We have to borrow this. This is way bigger and better than anything else anyone will find."

Oliver sighs and turns toward Mr. Johnson. "I'll get

the keys."

"You can leave that little car of yours here. Wouldn't hurt to sideline that symbol of capitalism for a bit." Mrs. Johnson winks at me. "It won't bother us. This is the most excitement we've had all week. Maybe all month!" She claps.

I look at Ollie, who's moving his hands in and out of his pockets. I know better than to ask him to be spontaneous or change up a plan. He's an accountant, for goodness sakes. But I can't resist this opportunity.

"I don't know, Dais. We're on a pretty tight schedule. We still have all these items to check off our scavenger hunt and then we will have to come back and get my car."

"Don't worry about your car. It'll be here waiting for you after all the wedding excitement," says Mr. Johnson, who seems to think this is the best idea since sliced bread.

"Come on, Oliver. Let's live a little. It'll be an adventure." I give his arm a little punch. "It'll be good for you."

He rolls his eyes and walks to the passenger side door. "Anything quirky about this vehicle we need to know before we leave?"

"I've been keeping her in good shape. Hoped Thayer would change his mind and come out to get her, but looks like that won't happen."

I turn the key and she sputters to life. I crank the window down and thank the Johsnons as we pull out of the driveway. I wave to the cows and will them to stand up.

"Now this is an unexpected treat!"

I give the bus some gas and watch the breeze move through Ollie's hair; I swear I see a smirk. The front seat's narrow enough that our elbows almost touch. Just another perk in this vintage treasure.

CHAPTER ELEVEN

OLIVER

"Thanks for changing the plans for me!" Daisy grins. "I'm DramaDaisy this weekend—first the airplane, then falling at The Old Owl, and now I'm borrowing a bus."

The bus sputters as we drive down the road. Daisy pats the dashboard. "Come on, Misty, you can do it."

"Misty?"

"Fog speaks to me. You can't see, and then all of a sudden you have visibility and clarity."

Just like Daisy to pick the perfect name for this vehicle and simultaneously give it a greater meaning. I put my head back on the seat. I'm certain my watch would give me a gold star for my heart rate at the moment. The breeze. The company. It's unwinding me. "You know, Dais, your chaos and drama help me breathe. You're the only kind of mess that makes sense to me."

She pushes my shoulder. "Aw shucks, Ol. If I didn't know better, I'd think our little kisses meant something to you."

If only she knew how much time I spend thinking about the few encounters my lips have had with hers. About how the disorder that follows her around is a balm for my soul, which has only craved order up until now. I'm cheering as her good vibes kick my meticulously arranged plans to the curb.

"Okay," I say, changing the subject. "Let's go to Island Grocers and see if we can find someone to talk to for some marital advice."

"Ohhh! Great idea!"

I give her directions—turn right, then motion straight ahead.

Daisy's driving Misty like she's a precious jewel—slower than the speed limit, cautious with her spacing between vehicles, and taking every corner with a delicate turning radius.

"You and Misty may have to move with a little more expedience."

She shrugs and checks her side mirror and then her rearview mirror. "I'm not about to let anything happen to Misty under my watch, Ol. That would certainly bring bad karma."

She has a point. Finding parking in the overly crowded parking lot is its own adventure because Daisy's hesitant to squeeze Misty between two cars.

"Pull through the parking lot and into one of the boat trailer spots on the street."

She does as I suggest and gives the steering wheel a kiss before she closes the door.

Within three minutes of walking in, we run into Mrs. Harris, my third-grade teacher, in the frozen food aisle. Now we're making up time.

"Perfect," I say to Daisy. "Mrs. Harris, would you

mind giving us your best wedding advice on video for a scavenger hunt we're doing for Jac?"

Mrs. Harris stops her cart. "Oh my goodness. Of course. I would do anything for that dear girl and her happy wedding."

"Great." I pull out my phone. "Mrs. Harris, what's your best piece of marital advice for my sister Jac?"

"Well, that's easy. Costumes. Plenty of costumes." She giggles, and I turn off the phone.

I grit my teeth and smile. The words hit me like an errant dodgeball to the face—unwelcome and traumatic. Daisy thanks her while I stand frozen, wishing we'd never asked the question.

As we're walking out to the car, I shiver.

"You okay?" asks Daisy.

"Yeah, I just can't stop thinking about the dress-up box Mrs. Harris had in her classroom. Like, did she take that home on weekends? All I keep thinking about is the felt pilgrim hat from the Thanksgiving Day play. Not exactly romantic! "

Daisy reaches in her bag and pulls out a small bottle of something. "Here. Put some on your wrists and take a whiff."

"What is it?" I unscrew the top.

"A clarifying blend of rosemary and eucalyptus oils. It will help clear your mind of your horrifying images." She winks, and I give it a go.

"We need to find the albino deer," Daisy says as she coaxes Misty to life.

"The deer's impossible to find, and we'll wreck our schedule trying." Plus, if we see it and she looks at me with those irresistible eyes, I'm not sure I'll be able to resist the urge to kiss her again.

"But if we search for it, we're liable to find another animal anyway."

She has a point, so I direct Daisy toward the Grand Greensea Forest. There's so little room in Misty that I can practically feel the hairs on her arm when the breeze blows. Everything in me leans toward her, even though I know I shouldn't.

The second we step out of the car, we're wrapped in the peace of birdsongs and a welcome rustle of leaves through the trees.

As soon as we're on the trail, Daisy tilts her head to the sky like she's sunbathing—only there isn't any light filtering through the canopy. She takes a deep breath and another and reaches her arms up like she's doing a sun salutation. She catches me looking at her and says, "Letting them know how blessed I am to be in their presence."

I'm assuming the "them" she speaks of are the trees, but I'm really not one hundred percent sure.

Do I tell her how lucky I am to be in her presence? I shake my head and continue to walk to the place we're most likely to see the albino deer—where the streams cross and create a little rock bed.

The single-track path is quiet as we walk toward the water, giving me more time to think about ways to expand the definition of platonic friendship.

When we get to the crossing, we find a spot behind a tree to sit out of view, hiding us from any wildlife that may appear.

I start to whisper and Daisy puts her finger to my mouth and shakes her head. I resist every urge to run my lips across the reprimanding digit.

We're so close to each other. Practically on top of one

another. I breathe her in, and something in me settles.
Her hair smells like a bouquet of Burning Man goodness.
This is my moment of Zen.

We crouch behind the tree in silence for what seems
like an eternity, but is more like twenty minutes. If we
don't move on, we'll never complete our tasks. I know I'm
not supposed to care about our schedule, but this idle time
won't help us win.

I nudge Daisy's side. "We've got to go."

"Five more minutes."

Before I can respond, a crow swoops low in front of
us. I instinctively raise my phone.

"That better not be our wild animal submission,"
Daisy says and gets up, already heading back to the trail
with her shoulders slumped. "We need something rarer
than a crow in order to win."

She picks up her pace and I reach for her arm. I catch
a glimpse of her eyes—shiny with tears.

"Dais, what's going on?" I keep my hand wrapped
around her forearm.

She pulls it away and gives her eyes a quick wipe.
"Nothing. It's just—the money would really help me out."

Things are worse for her than she's been letting on.

"Talk to me. I run numbers for a living."

Daisy opens Misty's door and slumps down in the
seat. I follow suit, jumping in the passenger seat and
without thinking put a hand on her leg—and then pull it
away when sparklers start to ignite my insides from the
warmth of her thigh.

"I'm really happy to take a look at your financial situation. It's probably not that bad," I mutter. My eyes looking
straight ahead.

"Ol, the thing is, there's nothing to take a look at. I'm

broke. I hoped I'd get one or two of the gigs that I'd sent proposals for, but nada. At this rate, I'm going to have to move in with my parents when I get back from the wedding."

The words drop like a lead balloon. I want to solve all her problems. Immediately. But she's not asking for that—she's just letting me see what's going on.

"Misty's the first good thing that's happened to me." Her shoulders sink even further down in her seat. "And the two hundred and fifty dollars, well, it won't change my situation, but it wouldn't hurt."

If we win, of course, I'll give her the entire amount.

"Well, let's go win this thing!" I can't fix everything, but I can help her win this. "We're halfway through the challenge. I bet we can reenact some of their story pretty easily and take care of another one."

"Didn't Jac and Johnny kiss on the rocks during the fireworks?" Daisy asks.

"Yeah, that's where that damn picture that was splashed all over the tabloids was taken." Not the happiest moment in hindsight because of the heartache that ensued afterward, but definitely a memorable one.

"Let's recreate their kiss!" Daisy's mood has changed. She's excited and has already thrown the bus into reverse and started to drive away. But I'm stuck on the let's recreate the kiss part.

"Just tell me how to get there," she says.

"Take a right at Goat Rock and then drive for about a mile."

"Let's take a picture of Goat Rock for good measure! That's a great landmark."

She's right, it is. The rock was painted by a bunch of high school seniors on the island's annual Paint Night.

Seniors paint their names in front of their houses in the middle of the night. They always paint something extra and one year it was Goat Rock—a rock that people believed was in the shape of a goat. Now it's an island legend and painted every few years to maintain its look.

"STOP!" I yell, and Daisy hits the brakes as a grey furry animal lumbers across the road.

"What is that?" asks Daisy.

"I don't know! A goat? A donkey? Maybe a llama?" I can't remember any of the basic farm animals, but this one seems to be a combination of at least three.

"Take a picture of it!" Daisy rolls down the window to get a better view.

I grab my phone, lean over Daisy, and snap a pic, then a video. A black matte Cybertruck comes up on the other side of the road and honks at the animal, causing it to dart off into the woods.

Tool. Scared away the animal—and I won't pretend I didn't enjoy my arm grazing Daisy's chest.

Daisy claps her hands and squeals. "Check another thing off the list! I bet it's the llama that bit Sam!"

I hate to break it to her, but whatever we just saw may not qualify as a wild animal. But for now, we'll take whatever we can get.

As we head to our next destination, we pass Goat Rock and take a few pictures. Then we pull up to the spot on the bay where Johnny and Jac kissed as they watched the fireworks. It's a secluded little beach area that offers a view of Seattle and the ferry on its hourly runs. It's definitely on my list of top ten favorite spots on Greensea.

We're in full-on golden hour—the best time of day on Greensea. Mt. Rainier glows and the water glimmers.

"Let's go down there and sit on the rocks and pretend

we're Jac and Johnny." Daisy points to the rows of boulders before us.

We're actually doing this. Kissing on the rocks. Good
idea? Probably not, but it's all for the game, I remind my
nerve endings.

Stepping over the first set of boulders, I turn back and
offer Daisy a hand. Her strappy flip flops were not made
for climbing. We nestle down in a sandy spot, while my
knees send out an S.O.S. that they're too close to a
forbidden object. Daisy props her phone on a rock and
hits record.

Her fingers brush mine for a second. My heart rate's
racing like it's on a scavenger hunt of its own. I'm short-
circuiting internally, and she's as calm as a dog in the sun
sitting next to her best friend's brother.

Daisy cocks her head to the side and turns toward me.
Her lips are a quarter of an inch away.

How far will we take this?

It's just pretend, right?

I can smell her breath and feel her heat. She glances
at my lips and the air shifts. It's taking every ounce of self-
control just to sit there.

But Daisy leans closer, bridging the gap, and takes my
lips with hers. I open my mouth, welcoming her with my
tongue. I'm lost in the pleasure that's Daisy and all her
dreamy benevolence. Holding the nape of her neck with
my hand, I lean into the kiss.

A ferry horn blasts in the distance, the waves lap on
the rocky shoreline, and every ounce of me wants to
believe it's real, but I know there's a camera recording this
for a family treasure hunt. Even though it's make-believe,
I still want to bottle whatever it is that Daisy stirs up
inside of me and save it for a rainy day.

I pull my head away first and reach for the phone.

"Daisy, that didn't feel pretend," I whisper my confession.

"We're just recreating the kiss, Ol," she says in a breathy voice. "That's all."

Right. Confirmation. It was all for the show.

But she won't quite meet my eyes. And I swear there's a tremble in her smile.

I have no idea how I'll sit at a rehearsal dinner and a wedding with my family acting like I didn't feel anything when deep down my heart's screaming for more of her. It may have been make-believe, but it had consequences in my heart.

CHAPTER TWELVE

DAISY

"Four hours and fifty-two minutes!" Miles stops a timer as Oliver and I arrive at the front door.

"Are we first?" I ask while I say a silent prayer to all the gods of Greensea.

He laughs. "Darling, the first team arrived three hours ago. You are dead last."

Of course we're last. I need to start carrying an umbrella with the black cloud over my head. I should have known this was going to happen. No money for me to stave off the bill collectors. My head falls, and Oliver puts a hand on my shoulder.

"Don't despair. Who knows, you may be the most original," says Miles.

My shoulders grow a little taller. "We did borrow a bus. I bet no one else did that!"

"No, I think you're right about that. I don't believe anyone borrowed anything larger than a bread box." Miles looks at his phone before he gathers his things. "Goodnight! Don't forget to send your video clips to the special wedding email. You never know what might happen."

I plop down at the island and send all the videos before it gets any later. It's a long shot, but maybe there's a consolation prize we don't know about.

The Sherman house is quiet. I grab a leftover club sandwich from the fridge and walk out onto the deck, sitting in one of the lounge chairs facing the bay. It's dark, but the faint outline of the trees and the glistening bay makes me smile.

My knees are still wobbly from my day. I need to reframe my bad luck narrative and focus on the magic Greensea dropped in my lap. My dream vehicle appeared like a manifestation off my vision board. And the magical kiss—even if it was one-sided—will live on repeat in my mind for a long time.

Before I even take a bite of my sandwich, Ollie sits next to me.

"I'm sorry we didn't win," he says.

"Me too," I sigh.

"I had fun, though." He reclines his lounger a notch.

"I did too. Sorry, I was a little over the top. Most people probably borrowed a bracelet or a pair of earrings—I made us borrow a bus."

Ollie laughs. "Whenever I'm with you, I never know what's going to happen."

He's quiet for a second, and I'm nervous about what he might say next. "But somehow, it doesn't stress me out the way things usually do. Numbers are predictable; people aren't...but when we're together, the unpredictability feels just right."

For the second time today, Ollie tells me my chaos isn't making him crazy. If I didn't know better, I'd think his words were a declaration of sorts. That may be the kindest thing anyone has ever said to me. Lately, my quirks—things I thought were my brightest bits—have been met with side eyes and sighs and not love.

A shiver runs through me and it has nothing to do with the breeze coming off the water. I reach for a beach towel that's slung over one of the deck railings to wrap around myself.

"You're a unicorn then," I answer. "I'm pretty sure my unconventional ways put most people, including your sister, into a mild state of panic."

"I don't think you stress Jac out. She may not understand everything you do, but she loves everything about you."

Hearing Ollie say all this has my heart doing cartwheels. But it's not like the kiss on the beach is indicative of our future. It's some made-up improv exercise I'm playing around with, but it did get my hopes up and my heart is bound to get crushed.

I gaze up at the sky, needing a little grounding. The stars pop on Greensea even with the close proximity to Seattle. "It's so peaceful out here," I murmur to the constellations more than anything else.

"I kind of forget what it's like to be on Greensea when I'm in the city." Oliver lounges with his hands behind his head.

A frog croaks in the distance. A coyote howls.

Wait a second. I blink my eyes. It can't be. It's happening right here.

"Look!" I whisper-yell, pointing to a faint puff of a cloud in front of us that dances through the sky. "Northern Lights! Right here over your house on Greensea!!"

"I must be blind," he says as he squints.

I grab my phone and take pictures. I shove the photo in his face. It's purple and the most vibrant green in a chevron pattern across the sky.

"See, the camera captures light over time. It makes the colors darker than what our naked eye can see."

He looks, hands my phone back, and watches the sky. "There's a patch right there. Do you think that's it?"

"Looks like it!"

He takes his phone out of his pocket and snaps a picture. "That's amazing. Pure magic." He looks, takes another picture, and then looks again.

I squint my eyes and watch the clouds dance and take pictures on my phone. Adam went all the way to Alaska for what he could've seen right here on this wondrous island.

The lights dance through the sky for a good thirty minutes, the colors becoming more vibrant to the naked eye, and then it dissipates like it never happened.

I turn on my side in my chair and look at Oliver, unable to stop grinning.

"Have you noticed that whenever we're together magical things happen?" I ask my voice dancing in the air. "The albino deer. Misty. Northern Lights."

As if the fairy lights pop on and show me the way, the bubbles inside of me rise up and take over. I reach out and grab his arm like I'm trying to catch the sparkly moments and hold on to them in midair before they fly away.

"They sure do." He lets me hold him like he wants to savor the moment as much as I do.

We're both quiet for a minute. Oliver tucks a piece of hair behind my ear and touches his finger to my lips, tracing the outline. My body leans toward him like a flower reaching for the sun. I move closer, and just as our lips nearly meet, my chair tips sideways. I burst out laughing as Oliver catches me and pulls me onto his chair, our bodies plastered together.

This time, he initiates the kiss. His lips caress mine before his tongue plunges inside my mouth. One arm wraps around my back pulling me closer and the other presses into my hip.

This. This is what I've wanted. What I've been trying not to want. But now it's here, and I'm terrified it's too good to be true.

Everything is perfectly aligned.

Oliver pulls his head back. "I've been wanting this for years."

What? Years?

My heart pops like a cork in a bottle of champagne.

He wants this too. His breath is warm on my cheek and his words are music to my ears.

Today on the beach, I could have sworn it was more than a reenactment. The energy between us didn't feel one-sided, and now I have the confirmation I need.

It's like the stars are saying we should be together. Like all the magic bucket list things appear when we're together, are giving us a metaphorical thumbs-up. It's like I'm going to find a four-leaf clover every time we're near each other. And I've never felt like that with anyone else.

"You've wanted this too?" I ask in a whisper.

"Hasn't it been obvious? I fall over myself to spend more time with you."

True, but I thought it was only because he was a nice guy.

He leans in and kisses me again. I run my hand across

his chiseled bicep. His fingers graze the small of my back, igniting a shiver that zips right through me.

This is for real and not because of a task on a scavenger hunt.

"Ol?"

He stares into my eyes.

"Could this ever be something?"

"I think it already is," he says.

My heart sings. Our noses rub and we kiss again.

I can already hear Jac's voice in my head—her one rule echoing like a fire alarm. No falling for her brothers. But this is different than my other relationships. It's deeper and built on something beyond just physical attraction. And because of that, it will work. Besides, I hate to think our friendship couldn't withstand a breakup. Jac should have enough faith in me that I'm not going to do anything to hurt Ollie on purpose. If things were to end, it would be with mutual respect.

Maybe the rule isn't meant for now because maybe this isn't falling—it's landing.

"Should we wait 'til after the wedding to tell everyone?" I ask.

"That's probably best. We can enjoy ourselves in secret until then." His hand runs along my chin.

If Oliver's willing to ignore the Sherman family rule, so am I.

"Are you sure you're okay with keeping this a secret?" I ask.

"Only for a few more days. Then we'll have Tippy announce it in GG." He laughs.

More music to my ears. My phone pings, and I glance at it to make sure it's not Jac from inside the house.

Mom: Something's going to happen.
Call me.

Not now, Mom. I wrap my leg around Ollie and he presses into me. His hand grazes my bra strap, sending my body into overdrive. Every part of me wants Oliver Sherman. I swivel my hips into him, and he groans.

"Daisy Bennett, I want you and all your chakras."

"I want you too, even with all those spreadsheets, Ol. But let's wait. I want to devour you when we're not hiding on a lounge chair at your parents' house."

His breath tickles my ear.

"I'll wait for whatever you want, Dais, as long as it means I can have you."

———

Two things race through my mind when I wake up; our for-real kiss and my mom's text. One still sends tingles down my spine, and the other is like a pebble in my shoe. Whether Mom meant to scare me or not, she did, and I'm not sure I can deal with her premonitions at the moment. My plate is full with forbidden kisses and borrowed buses, plus my best friend's wedding.

I check my phone to make sure there aren't any other ominous messages. Just one from Adam with a picture of the Northern Lights in Alaska—ours were better—and a message that says he misses me. That's another messy sentiment I don't have time to deal with.

I creep upstairs, nervous to see Ollie. What if he regrets our kiss? What if he's decided I'm not worth it? The smell of his aftershave—a mix of citrus and sea salt—

lingers on my skin. Mental note: Find out what it is and bathe in it.

But it's not Ollie in the kitchen; it's Jac. Even scarier.

"Hey!" She's literally jumping up and down.

"Hi," I say and open the refrigerator, grabbing the orange juice. I'm afraid our stolen kisses are tattooed on my face.

"Did you and Oliver enjoy the treasure hunt?"

"Umm...yeah. Great event. Still lost."

Jac hands me a glass from the cabinet.

"How do you know?"

"Well, everyone was asleep by the time we finished. Kind of a dead giveaway."

Jac chuckles and nods.

"Do you know anything about the bus in the driveway?"

I take a huge gulp of juice. "It's our something borrowed, old, and blue."

"You borrowed a whole bus?" Jac squeals. "That's...so extra! And so you! You've always wanted one."

"Yeah," I say, wishing it was mine for good. "Misty and I are BFFs."

"Misty?"

"The bus!"

Jac touches my arm. "You know we're best friends forever...even when I'm married. Not even a bus can come between us!"

I smile. That may not be the case when she finds out about Ollie and me.

"What do we have planned today?" I ask, stealing a glance at the door, hoping Ollie doesn't walk in. I'll never be able to hide my feelings if she sees us together.

Jac grabs my hands. "I have the most gigantic favor ever!"

"Lay it on me!" I say with a big sigh of relief that my face isn't revealing that I've been making out with her brother.

She pulls out a piece of paper she's ripped out of a spiral notebook.

"Johnny and I need to do last-minute fittings, make sure the license is in order, and check everything else off this list. But I need someone I trust to go to the ferry and help pack the gift bags. I want them to be a surprise for all the guests, and you're the absolute best person for the job."

"I'm your girl! Misty and I are at your service."

"You are the best best friend in the entire world. I texted Oliver, and he's going to be your partner in crime."

Insert awkward silence. I take another sip of juice.

She gives me a big hug. She takes a big sniff. "You've been spending so much time with Oliver that you're beginning to smell like him."

I choke on my juice, take a couple of steps back, and let out a cackle. Jac eyes me. "Lay off the ashwagandha. We need you at full force over the next few days!"

"Will do!" I yell and walk out the front door.

GREENSEA GAZETTE

Islanders,

Looks like the wedding is not the only historical event taking place on Greensea this weekend! Did you see the Northern Lights? They were magical! It is the peak of the sun's eleven-year solar cycle, so it is to be expected. But it seems like a harbinger of good things to come.

Let them eat cake! Jac and Johnny tried a dozen baked by Violet VanWoosen herself. Violet's a recent grad of a farm-to-table baking school and has a cake baking business in an ADU on her parents' property. She's second-generation Greensea and we're happy to see her making a name for herself. Picking the cake was the toughest decision for the happy couple. Chocolate, red velvet, carrot, champagne, lemon, white, yellow. You name it, they tried it. They narrowed it down to three cakes; a decadent chocolate filled with espresso buttercream and flavored with a touch of local Greensea whiskey; a carrot cake made from local hand grated carrots and a vegan cream cheese frosting in the layers (*I know! I can't wait to taste it either*); *and a white cake made with Greensea flour and butter from— you guessed it—Greensea cows. with layers of local fresh strawberry cream in between the cake layers for the top tier. Each tier will be covered in fondant and decorated with artwork representing their ferry tale, topped off by a handmade sugar sculpture of the rockstar and his fiancée.*

Do not worry! Violet plans to bake an assortment of cupcakes in all the flavors so each guest may try each cake.

Our other island tour-de-force, Felicia Higgins, has been scouring the island collecting flowers of all types for days. Have any extra? Drop them off at the ferry dock. We can't wait to see what she does with the random assortment of local blooms.

When I say every detail of this wedding has been planned with the utmost care, I mean it. Kudos to Miles and his team for hiring young, up-and-coming entrepreneurs on the island. It will be an event written about in the annals of Greensea history. Special thanks to islander Amanda Willows, for jumping in and helping him source every-thing on Greensea. Her PTO skills have come in handy outside of the school walls.

Since the royal wedding is making Greensea an even more popular destination, we need to keep putting our best foot forward. Recent college grads are running a pedal pub, to and from the ferry. It's fun, summery, and in the spirit. But the high school kids who wanted in on the action, your creation doesn't meet the bar. Charging tourists to ride on the back of your tandem bike? Nah, that's not the look!

And according to Mayor Nickerbottom, it violates city ordinance 75.3.

With the countdown to the most decadent island event on, just a reminder to keep it classy, Greensea!

xoxo,

GG

CHAPTER THIRTEEN

OLIVER

I do a mental happy dance as I'm coming back from my run and I see her speed-walking up the driveway dressed in loose-fitting plaid pants and a tiny tank top.

"Where are you off to in such a hurry?" I ask.

"I wanted to escape so Jac wouldn't see us together and since I didn't see you in the house, I figured you were running."

I'm a record on repeat when it comes to my schedule. If it's morning, I run. Something inside me flips that she noticed.

"Why are you afraid for Jac to see us? As the Best Man and Maid of Honor, it's going to be hard to hide from the bride on her wedding weekend."

Daisy's eyes are gigantic, and her hair is wild.

"I know that but we can at least limit the times we're alone with her. She's my best friend and if there isn't anything else to distract her, she'll sense the energy between us in a second."

I nod my head and she waves a piece of paper in front of my face. "But time for our marching orders."

"First things first." I pull her behind a tree.

I shouldn't. Not here. But she smells like oranges and trouble and I can't resist taking her lips with mine and kissing her.

"Good morning," I mumble.

"Good morning to you." She lands two soft, quick kisses on my lips.

I wrap my arm around her back. "You always do this," she says.

"Do what?"

"Make it hard for me to breathe."

We kiss again, exchanging everything behind the tree that we can't share in the house.

Daisy's hands touch my back. "You're sweaty."

"What did you expect? I was out for a run."

"Jac told me I smelled like you."

"Sweat and pent-up desire?"

"Ew! No!" She takes a step back.

"What did you say?"

"Nothing. Almost spit up my orange juice though."

A car comes up the driveway, and I pull her back toward me to ensure we're hidden behind the tree.

"Jac and Johnny," I say as the taillights pull away. "Glad they're too occupied to notice us."

"I'd love to find something special for Jac in town. Do you think we can do that before we pack the gift bags?" Daisy asks.

"Of course," I say, and we walk down the driveway.

———

Long planks of painted white wood stretch out in front of us. Soft harp music emanates from speakers. Glass cases trimmed with driftwood hold every type of crystal. The ceiling's draped with herbs, maybe lavender, and fairy lights. Daisy takes a deep breath.

"Palo Santo. I think I've walked into the mothership! Why hasn't Jac brought me here before? Is this store new?" Daisy asks.

The person behind the counter answers, "No, we've been here since 1982. I took over five years ago."

"Hey, Meredith," I say to one of my brother's old classmates sitting behind a large glass cabinet, working on her laptop.

She lets out a sigh before she speaks. "Hey, Oliver. Ready for the big wedding?"

"Just about," I answer. "How are things in the rock business?"

"Gems and crystals." She takes off her large black glasses. "Can't the Sherman brothers remember that?"

"Apologies. How's business with the 'gems and crystals'?"

"It's ok."

"Anything I can help with? I do all the books for Cedar & Fern, Sherman's Shellfish, and Applehill Farm."

"Thanks, but it's not the numbers that are the problem."

Daisy pokes around the cases of crystals. Out of the corner of my eye I see her picking rocks up, closing them in her fist, and then setting them down.

"What's the problem then?"

"My sister's pregnant and was put on bedrest. She needs help with her toddler, so she asked me to come.

Trying to call in my summer help to see if they can cover for me here. No luck yet."

"Excuse me," says Daisy. "I'm looking for a wedding gift. Do you have any ideas?"

Meredith walks over to a gigantic pink rock in the center of one of the tables and picks it up. "This is a perfect wedding gift."

She hands it to Daisy. It's solid. A hefty piece. I'm not sure why anyone would buy a rock that size.

"Rose quartz...love and compassion. It symbolizes everything I want for Jac and Johnny. How much is this?"

Of course...Daisy wants it.

"This piece is two hundred dollars," says Meredith.

Daisy hands it back to her. "If I knew whether we'd won the scavenger hunt, I could just put it on hold." She sighs and looks around the shop. "Any chance you'd be willing to barter?"

"Dais, remember, people outside the Burning Man group don't barter."

"Quiet, Oliver." Meredith turns to Daisy. "What'd you have in mind?"

Daisy rummages through her oversized bag. A stray feather I'd hoped had disappeared jumps out. She pulls out an intricately knit scarf. "This is all I have with me right now." She looks around. "Do you need any graphic design work?"

No wonder Daisy's business isn't going like she'd hoped. She gives her talents away. "Dais, I'll buy the rock —sorry!" Meredith's shooting daggers my way. "I mean crystal. You can pay me back."

"Ollie, I can't be indebted to you. It would tie our cords together in the wrong way and drain our energy."

Huh. I thought we both wanted to "tie our cords" together.

"I want to keep our auras clean and watch them meld in other ways," Daisy continues.

Meredith looks between us like a bobblehead and shakes her head. "I don't want to know. I don't need any design work, but I do need someone to manage the shop for a few weeks while I help my sister out."

"Me!" Daisy shouts and raises her hand. "I'll do it! I'm your girl."

Now I'm the bobblehead looking between Meredith and Daisy. "Wait! What? You live in San Francisco," I remind her.

"I'm portable. I can do it." Daisy turns to Meredith. "I'll start after the wedding."

It all happens so fast, it makes me dizzy. Major decisions are made faster than I can spit out any words.

Meredith wraps her in a hug, places the crystal in tissue paper, and sets it in a box. Meredith and Daisy shake and she agrees to report to work on Monday morning.

As soon as we're outside the store, I question her. "Dais! You just took a job on Greensea?"

I mean, yeah, it means she's sticking around a bit longer—but who just takes a job in another state on a whim? It's peak Daisy. I made a spreadsheet of optimal training windows before picking a date for my Ironman. Daisy probably thinks Excel is a new band at Lollapalooza.

"I know! Isn't it amazing!"

I'm part flabbergasted, part terrified, and part in awe as we walk on the sidewalk toward the harbor and the ferry.

"What are you going to do about your apartment in San Francisco?"

"My landlord will be happy to see me go." She shrugs. "I was already thinking I would have to move in with my parents."

Nora Cunningham yells, "Have fun at the wedding, Oliver" from across the street.

I half-wave to Nora. "What about all your stuff?"

"This is only temporary. I'll figure it out. But Mom and Dad can take care of it for me for a bit."

I stop my mail when I go out of town for a week and worry about watering the orchid on my kitchen island.

"Your clients?"

"Nonexistent."

"What will your parents think?"

"They'll be thrilled that I've inherited their wandering spirits."

Daisy stops in her tracks as Clyde the Bike Cowboy rides down Main Street in full costume—hat, vest without a shirt, chaps, and boots.

"This place is amazing. Taking this job is the best decision I've ever made." She's as giddy as a champagne toast.

I've seen Clyde ride down Main Street a hundred times, but never did it make me want to stay on Greensea forever. Leave it to Daisy to see the local Bike Cowboy as a cosmic sign.

But the real game changer? What was shaping up to be a long-distance thing may now be a real-life possibility. Although I hope we don't make any more life decisions as we walk to the ferry to do the actual job Jac asked us to do.

We're greeted by buckets of wildflowers dropped off by local gardeners on the deck of the ferry. It makes me happy to see how Greensea-ers have truly come through for Jac.

"Anything we can help with, Felicia?" I ask the florist. Felicia and I went to school together. She stayed on Greensea and opened Ferry Florals. It's at the entrance to the ferry terminal and the perfect spot to grab some flowers before you get home.

"Not unless you can snap your fingers and turn all of these into centerpieces," she sighs.

"There's something poetic about all these flowers waiting to be chosen to celebrate love, don't you think?" Daisy asks.

"Hi, I'm Felicia." Felicia sticks out her hand while Daisy goes in for a hug.

"I'm Daisy." Her face lights up.

"Innocence, purity, and new beginnings. I like you without even knowing you," says Felicia.

Daisy giggles.

"I speak fluent flower." Felicia shrugs.

Another language I don't speak but am willing to learn.

"Dais, we better get to work. We need to pack all the bags before we go to the rehearsal."

"It was nice meeting you." Daisy touches Felicia's forearm and we walk away.

The interior of the old ferry has been transformed. All the booths have been removed and replaced with round tables and chairs. Bell Meadowcroft and a few women I recognize as Mom's friends are decorating one of the tables with seashell candelabras encircled by a ring of moss. Daisy walks over to the table and claps her hands to her face.

"How meaningful and beautiful! The juxtaposition of

new beginnings surrounded by serenity."

All I can see is a bunch of shells and ground covering. Somehow Daisy makes even that sound poetic.

"Thanks for seeing my vision," says Bell, our Greensea expert on tabletop design. Everyone meets Daisy's positive attitude with a similar energy.

We meander toward the galley watching every surface being covered in tulle and shades of green.

"It's a magical wonderland," Daisy says, twirling as we walk.

The ferry galley's filled with boxes marked *swag*. I pick through the first set, which is filled with homemade marshmallows, bouquets of twigs, handmade chocolate, and graham crackers.

"Oh my gosh! Are these the all-natural, organic, dairy-free marshmallows I've heard about?" Daisy asks.

"It's Greensea, so that sounds about right."

The next set of boxes has green plaid blankets. Nothing more American than s'mores and more British than a tartan blanket.

Daisy takes out a blanket and wraps it around her shoulders.

"Divine!"

The green brings out the gold flecks in her eyes. She's so happy, enjoying everything as it comes.

"The swag is next level!"

She's right. They've spared no expense to make this wedding one-of-a-kind.

I open the last set of boxes—cream canvas totes with green handles, tagged with a note that says, "You're ferry special to us."

I survey the space and try to figure out the most efficient way to get this done. But when I turn around

Daisy's unpacked the totes and they're strewn across the floor of the galley.

"What the hell?" I practically get the shakes looking at the mess and don't tamper my reaction.

"What? I'm getting all the bags out and clearing their energy."

"Canvas bags don't have energy."

Daisy tilts her head and squints. "Au contraire, Oliver. Everything has energy."

"Can we at least examine them on the counter?" At a minimum, I can compromise.

I take the bags to the counters meant for trays and set them up around the galley. Crisis averted. "First, we'll place a blanket in each. Then we'll add the s'mores."

Daisy walks to the far end of the galley. "Okay. I'll start from this side."

"No!" My voice is more exuberant than I intend. Daisy looks at me with wide eyes.

"Ol, you have more directions than a game of Monopoly."

I roll my eyes. "I'll carry the box and you place the blanket in the bag."

Of course Daisy has to do it with her style. She places a blanket in the bags out of order. It works. Each time she does it, she cocks her head and gives me a smirk.

"Just messing with you. You show love by how carefully you do things," she says.

No one's ever seen me and accepted me like this. My habits are usually met with rolled eyes, but Daisy meets them with love—even if she messes with me while she's doing it. It's like Valentine's Day, Christmas morning, and a perfectly salted ferry pretzel all wrapped up in one.

"How about we reward ourselves with an ice cream cone?" I ask not wanting the afternoon to end.

"Oliver Sherman! How did you know ice cream speaks to my soul?"

I laugh. I had no idea, but I'm wondering if there's anything that doesn't.

Seas the Scoop, right on Main Street, has the most creative ice cream names. Come to think of it, is there anywhere on Greensea that doesn't have unique names for their products? The island's is a mecca for word-smiths. *Chip! I missed the ferry* - vanilla chocolate chip with island fresh raspberry swirl. *The Great Dark* - triple chocolate with brownie chunks. *Green Monster* - mint chocolate chip. Today they're serving gnome cones in honor of the local garden gnome displays.

"How will I ever choose just one flavor?" asks Daisy.

"No need," says the teenager behind the counter. "We have a four-scoop sampler in a cone."

Daisy turns to me. "Want to share?"

Four scoops in a cone sounds messy but how can I resist? I nod and let her pick.

We find a bench under the Jac & Johnny banner stretching across the street and take turns licking our ice cream with the occasional nose brush when we both meet at the center at the same time. Sure we've been busy with wedding activities, but today seems like what normal life with Daisy would be like—unexpected and filled with joy. Somehow, even the mundane tasks are magical with her.

CHAPTER FOURTEEN

DAISY

"Why did the ferry break up with the tugboat?" Ollie asks as we walk into the rehearsal dinner at Fork & Stable.

"No idea. Why?" I ask.

"Too much emotional baggage."

I giggle and give Oliver's arm a little shove.

Tippy's walking toward us at a speed reserved for the Olympics. Her lips are pursed, and her hands are on her hips. Her face is the color of her hair. She stops us in the parking lot, not even giving us a chance to walk inside.

"I edited the video." She practically spits at us.

"What video?" Oliver asks.

"The scavenger hunt video, dummy!"

"Did we win?" I ask. "Yay!"

"No," she hisses.

Damn. "Was Mrs. Harris's part too much? We both cringed a little when we saw it. Oliver has PTSD thinking about the dress-up chest."

"No! That was typical Harris." She tightens her ponytail. Tippy assumes a drill sergeant position. "The cringey part was the two of you kissing on the beach!"

Oliver and I stop like we've been frozen in a game of freeze tag.

"Hahahahaha." My laugh sounds more like a Canada goose. "We were just acting out Jac and Johnny's first kiss."

"Acting my ass," accuses Tippy, pointing her finger at each of us. "I could see the fireworks going off."

"There weren't any fireworks," says Ollie. "That was the one thing we were missing."

Tippy cocks her head and rolls her eyes. "Metaphorical fireworks."

She looks at each of us, waiting for one of us to break. "I've been watching you guys and hearing rumblings about the two of you together from the moment you arrived on Greensea, Daisy. You two are just lucky I caught the video first and no one else saw it."

I scrunch up my shoulders, raise my eyebrows, and try to look innocent.

"It doesn't take a brain surgeon to see what's going on," says Tippy. "Sharing a cone at Seas the Scoop? What the heck?"

I look to my left and my right—nothing but bushes surrounding the parking lot. I could take off running down the street, but at this point, I'm not sure what good that would do me anyway. We're on an island and I'm at my best friend's wedding. I still can't resist the urge to flee.

"Nothing is going on," says Ollie. His hand brushes against mine. Is he apologizing for the lie or reminding me he's still there?

Nothing? My chest falls.

I turn my head and glare at him.

I mean, I know we're trying to hide it, but am I really nothing? I'm ready to dot my letters with hearts. I'll kiss him again right here and now to prove to all of Greensea I felt something. But instead, I cross my arms across my chest and let my heart deflate.

"I guess he's right, Tippy. Nothing is going on here." My voice is high and breathy. My heart is beating in my ears.

"No, no." He turns to me. "I don't mean nothing. You know what's in my heart."

Tippy puts her hands out in front of her. "Stop. I don't want to know anymore. This is not your weekend."

I'm not sure why I keep forgetting that. If Jac weren't in Wedding Bliss La La Land she'd have noticed and would be yelling at me.

"Honestly, I have no issue with the two of you hooking up. But Jac is going to have feelings," says Tippy.

"Are you using the video?" I ask.

"NO! Do you think I'm crazy?"

Thank goodness. Crisis averted.

"But I'm going to be watching the two of you very closely. I want to see ice coursing through your veins. None of that ooey-gooey love stuff between the two of you."

"We haven't done any of that in public," I say.

"Please! You'd have to be preoccupied not to see it. I saw the glances exchanged while you untangled the anklet. The heat flying off the two of you during the rhumba. All of it. You've got sparks. And take it from someone who tried to ignore the sparks, it won't work. Just stick yours in an ice bath until after the wedding."

Tippy walks away. My eyes meet Ollie's and something passes between us.

Ollie grabs my hand. "I'm sorry. I didn't mean to make you think that I regretted anything that happened. I just didn't think Tippy was the first person who should find out."

I get it. I'd be lying if I said it didn't hurt though. I nod. "Let's just get through the wedding." But my insides are screaming.

"Go ahead in without me," says Ollie. "I'm going to get something from the car."

With the weight of all my feelings on my shoulders, I walk through the parking lot to the rehearsal. Miles has transformed Fork & Stable into a whimsical mock-ferry wedding venue, complete with nautical touches and island charm. Following the rehearsal, he's planned a lively hoedown—because if there's one theme running through this wedding weekend, it's music, dancing, and a whole lot of joy.

I run into Jac as soon as I walk in the door—literally knock right into her, spilling her champagne.

"Oh my gosh! I'm so sorry!"

"Slow down!" She giggles and wipes the champagne away—not caring for a second. "Thank you sooo much for doing all that for me today. I don't know what I would do without you!"

She throws her arms around me.

"Anything for you!" I say as the barn door swings open and Ollie walks in.

"You two are the dream team! This wedding would be nothing without you!" Jac pulls Oliver into our hug.

His shoulder brushes mine. If Jac could sense the current between us would she still be smiling?

"Let's get this dry run started," says Miles, walking over with Sylviane and Tippy.

"Sam is going to step to the center of the altar. That will be the cue for the three groomsmen to line up on the steps—Oliver first, then Josh, then Dave. Johnny, you will stand in front of Sam and wait for your beloved bride."

Sam steps out and they all follow suit.

Miles lines up the rest of us. Tippy, followed by Sylviane, and then me. Tom and Jac stand behind us.

Miles whirls his fingers and music plays. Tippy begins the walk down the aisle.

"Slow down, slow down." Miles scoots next to her and emulates the big strides he'd like her to take instead of her normal fast pace.

Sylviane and I make it to our places without a reprimand.

Jac holds a bouquet of ribbons as she processes down the aisle with her dad. She's beaming and so is Johnny.

I catch Oliver's eye. For a second everything blurs—Jac's radiant smile, Johnny's glimmer, and Tippy's watchful eye. It's the two of us and all the big feelings we need to hide. We both look away.

"Fantastic!" Miles approaches. "Sam, Johnny, and Jac have all rehearsed their parts without all of you. After Johnny kisses his bride, they'll walk down the aisle, followed by the wedding party. Oliver and Daisy..."

Shit. I forgot we're going to have to walk down the aisle together. I picture Antarctica and glaciers of ice running over me.

"Tonight, we're going to skip the exit and move over to the rehearsal dinner and get ready for our hoedown!"

Do-si-do. Saved by the hay.

The wedding party is seated at a large round table

while Jac and Johnny are off on their own at a table for two.

As we're eating dinner—pulled pork sandwiches and coleslaw all locally grown—Miles gets up to speak.

"Good evening and welcome to the wedding of the century. First, a thank you to the fine people of Greensea for welcoming me into your open arms. And second, thanks to Johnny and Jac for being quite possibly the greatest couple ever."

The crowd claps and the couple clinks glasses.

"The Sherman and Nickels family went on a wedding scavenger hunt with their best mates yesterday. Many of you contributed to making these videos with your stories and your used items. Hope you enjoy this video."

Johnny's single Greensea Gal cues up at the same time as a picture of Jac giggling and then me singing. Gosh, I wish someone had told me I sounded like I was on the B roll for *American Idol*.

Next, we see the islanders dispensing their marital advice, "Never go to bed mad" and a montage of every-one's submissions. It's cute and sentimental and gives everyone a chance to oh and ah and dab cocktail napkins at their eyes.

Misty has a starring role—front and center as I drove her for the first time. I make a mental note to check out my camera roll and favorite the picture of Ollie and me waving from our seats.

Sam and Johnny reenact Sam being bit by the llama at the Fourth of July parade. Dave dons one of Tippy's blue pickleball skirts and she gasps from her seat as he sways his hips back and forth on the court. The clips are only a few seconds long and only three of us notice the part that's missing.

"And now, the winner of the scavenger hunt. Drum-roll please," says Miles and Sam obliges with some ad-lib drumming. "Tippy and Josh!"

My shoulders slump. I knew there was no chance for us to win, but I held a small amount of hope that Misty would give us a little edge. Tippy and Josh run up for their prize—the money—and toast as they taste their signature cocktail, The Tipsy.

I rub my mood ring to wipe away the jealousy.

"And the losers..."

Shit.

"With a time of four hours and fifty-two minutes, Oliver and Daisy."

We get a little whoop-whoop from the crowd before Miles continues.

"As losers, they will be couple number one in our square dance."

A bigger whoop-whoop. And all I can think is that I can't do it. I can't get up there and dance while all of them are watching me. Especially with Tippy's eyes on me. I know I'll unwittingly do something to give it away.

My palms start to sweat. Dancing with Oliver right now in front of everyone would be like juggling lit sparklers. I want it with every part of my being, but I need to run.

"No. No. Sorry. I can't square dance. The sacred geometry of the square doesn't match with my aura. It will, um, mess with my chakras. And no one wants that to happen."

Miles raises his eyebrows, and I beeline for my favorite safe haven—the bathroom—until the coast is clear and I can sneak out and spend the rest of the rehearsal at the bar.

———

"It's time for bubbles and besties!" Jac says as we walk into the house. An overgrown ice bucket sits on the island with a fancy French champagne chilling in it, and champagne flutes wait to be filled.

Jac reaches into the pantry and pulls out four gift bags —gosh, she went a little overboard with the gifts. She hands us each a soft brown leather tote filled to the brim— fluffy slippers, matching pajamas, face masks, eye patches.

"Jac! These are amazing," I say, laying out each item on the island.

"You can't resell any of this." Tippy gives me a side eye.

I cock my head and roll my eyes back at her putting on the slippers right away to make my intentions clear to Tippy.

"Popcorn time!" Jac calls out, ushering us like she's hosting a movie premier. On the coffee table, giant tubs of popcorn sit ready for us, nestled beside a Magic 8 ball ready to tell us our destiny.

Tippy grabs the Magic 8 ball. "Will I ever get a reality TV show filmed on Greensea Island?"

"Really, Tip?" asks Jac. "Still barking up that tree?"

"'Concentrate and ask again.'" Tippy scrunches her nose and closes her eyes, and then shakes the 8 ball again. "'Reply hazy. Ask again.'" She tosses it to Sylviane.

"Your turn, Syl!" Jac claps.

"Hmmm...I don't know what to ask!"

"Anything," says Tippy. "It's a freaking eight ball."

"Will Jac and Johnny live happily ever after?"

"That's a dumb question! It's the night before their wedding!" Tippy says through a mouthful of popcorn.

"It is decidedly so!" Sylviane smiles.

We all cheer.

"Your turn, Jac!" Sylviane hands it to her.

"Fine. I'll do it." Jac takes it and sets it in her lap.

Her energy shifts. The beaming bride glow has dimmed. Like suddenly she's afraid of the power of the twenty-sided die in the plastic ball.

"What's wrong?" asks Tippy.

"I'm afraid to ask what I really want to know." Jac's smile fades as she taps her fingers on the plastic ball.

"Wwwhaatt?" I ask. My face clenched.

"If everyone's here for the right reasons," Jac says.

My eyebrows soften. Phew.

"Don't be ridiculous. Sam and I have triple-checked the guest list. Everyone who will be on that ferry tomorrow will be there to see you marry your true love," says Tippy.

Jac's fingers grip the manufactured oracle. "Johnny told me about Arianna. Who would date my brother to get to Johnny's garbage?"

"She was a social climber and a fame seeker disguised as a plus one," says Sylviane.

Jac's nose crinkles. "Do you think Ollie is okay? He was quiet at the rehearsal tonight."

"He..." I begin.

But Tippy cuts me off.

"He's fine," she says with a glare.

I shake my head. I wasn't going to pour my feelings

over the popcorn like butter, even if that's what part of me wants to do.

"I don't think I can handle anyone else trying to hurt any person in this family."

Jac's words stick in my ears like pool water.

"The Shermans are fine," says Tippy. "Will you just ask that plastic ball a question? Let's not be all doom and gloom on the freaking night before your wedding!"

Jac's smile creeps back. "Is my best friend ever going to find love?" She gives it a shake, then holds the ball still and reads the die. "Closer than you think."

"Ohhhh!" Sylviane coos.

"Is it Adam?" Jac asks.

My grip on my champagne flute tightens. Tippy stuffs a fistful of popcorn in her mouth while she shoots poison darts at me with her eyes.

"No, no. I told you I friend-zoned him. We want different things, and he looked better on paper. Festival planner turned out to mean block party permitter."

"Then who could it be?" Jac puts a finger to her lips. "I have been noticing a glow about you, and it's not from Greensea Glam."

"Aaahhh." Tippy yawns. "Better get some beauty rest!"

Saved by Tippy. I mouth "thank you" when Jac isn't looking.

"Use your swag bags tonight to bring out your inner and outer glow!"

"You're too much, Jac," says Sylviane.

Jac grabs my arm as we walk downstairs to her room. "Who could the eight ball be talking about?"

I take the PJs out of the bag—a short set with unicorns and rainbows.

"Maybe a handsome stranger-to-me will sweep me off my feet at the wedding," I say, trying not to give anything away.

"Ohhh!"

I head to the bathroom before Jac can question me further. Jac's tucked in when I return.

"I'm so happy you're next to me." She spoons me and wraps me in a hug. "No matter what happens in our lives, promise me we'll always be friends. You're the only true and authentic person—apart from my family—in my life."

Shit. I'm so far from authentic at this moment.

I hate hiding things from her. We share everything. We even had a silent language across crowded parties in college. The mileage between us has brought a natural distance, but she's still a sister to me.

My phone pings.

> Mom: Embrace what appears in front of you.

"Who's that?" asks Jac.

"My mom. She keeps sending me messages and premonitions."

"Still? Even after nothing happened on the airplane?"

"Yeah, right now she sounds like a fortune cookie."

Jac rolls over. "That's better than the doomsday stuff."

It pings again.

> Oliver: Sleep well.

Three dots and my heart does a few backflips.

> Oliver: Can't get you out of my head.

And then a heart.

"What's she saying now?"

Lies on top of lies.

"Just saying goodnight."

I tuck my phone under my pillow and try to close my eyes, but nothing about me is ready to sleep.

CHAPTER FIFTEEN

DAISY

"Get up!" says Tippy bursting through the bedroom door. Her tone could cut rocks. I jump up, blink my eyes open, and swallow the taste of last night's champagne. Jac's not in bed next to me and I'm kind of worried that I didn't hear her get up.

But man, I sleep better in Greensea than anywhere else.

I look back at Tippy.

"What!? I didn't even look at Oliver last night."

"No! It's worse," she snarls.

Worse than me hooking up with Oliver? I sit up even straighter and look at Tippy.

"Apparently Tom woke up to a red sky."

I gasp. "Is there a fire?"

"No! You know...red sky in the morning, sailors take warning."

Oh no. Rain. I gasp again. "Old Man Johnson's cows

were lying down when we were on the scavenger hunt." I knew it was going to rain.

"And Sylviane said the birds are flying lower. To top it off, Barb's bunion hurts."

Rain is coming. I knew this was going to happen. Tippy's right—that's terrible news! I roll out of bed and throw on some clothes.

"What are we going to do? Is Jac freaking out?"

"She doesn't know yet. We've been whispering around her. Miles's working on it. Mayor Nickerbottom called in the Greensea Needlers."

"What are they going to do?" I ask.

"Who knows! Knit rain shawls for everyone?"

"That's not a thing." Even though anything seems possible on Greensea.

"No kidding, but I have no idea what he's thinking. Come talk with us in the kitchen."

The kitchen's turned into a war room. The guys have joined us from Sam's boat, looking surprisingly fresh. Oliver gives me a tiny head nod from the corner of the kitchen, causing my heart to flutter. He's so neat and polished in a dark green polo shirt and khaki shorts. I look away so I don't drool.

But I giggle when I see Johnny seated on a stool facing the fridge with a bandana tied around his eyes.

"What's with him?" I whisper to Sylviane.

"Bad luck to see the bride."

True, but it looks like he's been kidnapped and we're holding him for ransom.

The mayor walks in and speaks to Miles. If you didn't know what was going on, you'd think the big earthquake had hit and this was the command center.

Miles paces the room speaking to no one in French.

"You said the weather is nice after July fifth on Greensea!" Miles says to no one in particular.

"She looked out the window," whispers Tippy.

Jac's sitting motionless in a chair in the family room. We all steal glances at her over and over again like she's a china doll we're afraid will explode.

Barb busies herself chopping apples, strawberries, pears...whatever she can reach in the fruit bowl. Tom takes a banana away from her before she chops it—peel and all.

I catch a glimpse of Jac as she stands up and walks to the kitchen.

She takes a deep breath and folds her hands in prayer.

"It's okay." She smiles, and we all exhale the breath we didn't know we were holding. "It doesn't matter. Wet or dry, I still get to marry Johnny. The rain's just another part of the ferry tale."

Johnny stands up and walks backward toward Jac. And turns around as we all scream, "No!"

"I've got the bloody blindfold on!" And he touches Jac's face and finds her lips and kisses her.

"Let's do this thing!" Johnny spins around again in a signature rockstar move and feels his way back to the stool.

The room swings into motion as we all wait for marching orders.

"Josh and Sylviane, collect umbrellas from as many islanders as you can. Be sure they're labeled so it will be easy to find the owners," says Miles.

"But true PNWers don't use umbrellas," says Josh.

"With all your rain?" Miles is appalled.

"That may be true, but everyone still has one," says

Tippy. "I'll put out an emergency GG letting everyone know what we need."

"Josh, go to Cedar & Fern and grab anything we can use," adds Tom. Josh nods.

"Dave, grab buckets. We'll water the town garden with the rain collected on the ferry as a way to thank everyone for their help."

Miles smiles and looks at me and then Oliver. "You two go down to Greensea Sails and grab the extra rolls of canvas. Seamus is expecting you."

"And bring them to Laverne at The Salty Skein," adds Mayor Nickerbottom.

They're throwing us together again. How are we supposed to keep this a secret?

"No, no." I shake my head. "I'll go do it. Let Ollie stay here."

"Don't be silly, Dais. Let Ollie help you," Sylviane says. She has no idea what she's asking us to do. Tippy glares at me, and I think her eyes might melt my skin.

"No offense, darling Daisy, but you cannot carry the canvas on your own. Go load it into that vehicle you're borrowing and bring it to the lovely Laverne as fast as you can." Miles points at the door.

"Daisy, here's a raincoat. Don't want you to catch a chill." Barb drapes a black jacket over my shoulders.

Ollie and I head toward Misty without talking. I wouldn't put it past Tippy to be watching us out the window. But as soon as we close Misty's doors, Oliver looks at me.

"Hey," he says over the whir of the engine.

"Hey," I return. "Thanks for the text last night."

"Watching you from afar, not being able to hold your hand, touch your arm…it killed me."

My aura held an emergency meeting with my chakras and they all agree: Oliver Sherman makes them shine.

But it doesn't matter.

"It's already raining on Jac's wedding day. We can't do anything else to hurt her day," I say.

His chest rises and falls in the seat.

"Yeah, I guess you're right." He leans his head on Misty's window.

"At least my mom's texts have gone from apocalyptic to encouraging." I tell him about the last one.

Oliver looks at me. "Dais! She knew. Your mom saw this before we did!"

Something significant on the airplane was Oliver? Oliver, the logical one who doesn't believe in tarot cards and horoscopes, is pointing out the signs. How did I miss that?

My foot falls off the gas. The car behind me honks.

The love line on my palm burns. My mood ring turns magenta. My mom's premonition proves Oliver and I are meant to be.

My fingers ache to reach him. I want to hold his hand and not let go. But today is Jac's day, so none of that matters—at least until after the wedding.

"Let's just get this job done. Get our girl married. And then we can talk."

Oliver doesn't speak for the rest of the trip to pick up the canvas, which leaves me alone with my thoughts. All I want to do is call my mom to see what she thinks as the rain drums on Misty like a metronome counting down.

The sail shop is tucked in a group of warehouse buildings in the harbor. Seamus can't be missed waiting outside the shop in his bright yellow rain slicker and boots. He whistles as we pull up and his buddies carry the ream of canvas to Misty.

Sylviane was right. There's no way I could have handled the canvas on my own, and I'm very glad I have an assistant—and a bus.

We pull up to The Salty Skein and carry the ream inside. Black walls make the brightly colored skeins of yarn pop. Wicker light fixtures dangle like chandeliers. Boho rugs and a couch filled with quilts call up images of the coffee shop on *Friends*. I shake my head. Another magical Greensea destination.

Laverne and a dozen women sit around a long wooden table armed with gigantic needles and spools of thread.

"I've mobilized the team. We're ready for the challenge." I half-expect her to salute us.

"Thanks, Mrs. Nickerbottom. This means a lot to our family."

She touches Oliver's arm. "Anything for the Royal Shermans."

A tiny part of me wants to roll my eyes, but mostly I want to sign on the dotted line.

"What are you going to make?" My curiosity gets the best of me.

Laverne's eyes twinkle. "You'll see, sweetie, you'll see."

I can't wait to see what this team of fairy godmothers conjures up.

———

"Oh my gosh! Misty's windshield wipers don't go fast enough. It's raining cats and dogs."

There's a thunk. And then nothing. Then a thunk again. "What was that?"

"Not sure. Pull over here and I'll take a look."

I creep over to the side of the road and Ollie gets out. I throw up the hood on the old slicker and meet him at the back of the car.

"Misty has a flat tire," he says.

"Oh no! What do we do?"

Oliver looks at his watch. "We need to get back to the house to get ready for the wedding."

Shit. I have glam in thirty minutes.

"I'll call Mr. Johnson and see if we can exchange cars."

"But he'll be stuck with a flat tire."

"I'm certain Mr. Johnson will be able to change it in no time. Plus, he doesn't have to do his hair before the wedding."

"True." He's completely bald.

While Oliver makes the call, I huddle next to a tree. It's raining so hard it's not going to matter if they make a tent with the canvas; we'll still wash away on the ferry.

"He'll be here in a jiffy."

Oliver grabs my hand and we run back to Misty. We sit in the front seat, huddled in our raincoats. A chill runs through me even though it's July.

"Can't remember the last time I was in rain like this. Rain in the PNW tends to be a drizzle, not torrential." Oliver shakes his head in disbelief.

"Me either. Two years ago at Burning Man, there was a dust storm followed by a freak rainstorm while the Smothers Brothers played their ukuleles."

"That must've sucked."

"Nah. The rain's romantic."

"Romantic?" Ollie asks.

"Yeah. The smell of the wet earth. The chill with each drop. It all makes you want to get closer to whomever you're with. And then a kiss in the rain—gosh, they're the best. It's like kissing in the shower but you don't have to be self-conscious because you're fully clothed."

"I've never been kissed in the rain. Almost makes me want to go back outside." Oliver moves closer.

"Is that so?"

Our hoods meet.

"Yeah." He puts his hood down and cocks his head to the side. A raindrop falls on his upper lip. I wipe it away, and he holds my finger to his lips.

My phone pings, and a car door closes.

"Hello!" Mr. Johnson bellows.

Damn electric car. Never heard it coming. We jump out of the van to greet Mr. Johnson as he hands Oliver the keys.

"Believe you two have an important event to get ready for! I'll take it from here."

"Thanks!" we say in unison and run to the car. We're silent on the drive back. I'm not sure if it's because we're soggy and wet or because of the kiss we left hanging on the side of the road.

———

I dial my mom as soon as we get back to the house. I've ignored her for too long.

"It's about time, Daisy Lou!" Mom's full face fills my

phone screen. I'm glad I'm alone so no one hears my full name.

"I've been trying to get in touch with you," she continues.

"Sorry, Mom. I've been busy with wedding prep, but I need to ask you something."

"Go ahead! Ask me anything!"

"When you said something significant was going to happen on the plane, I figured you meant something bad..."

"I'm only seeing good things for you, honey!" She brings her eyeball close to the camera for emphasis. "Judging from the glow you're wearing on your cheeks, you've found the significant thing that makes you happy."

I shrug, not ready to admit it to her. "Greensea agrees with me."

"I can read you like a tea leaf, Daisy! You're in love!"

I hesitate. Love is a strong word.

"You don't have to answer. I see it, and this one's for real."

I twist a curl around my finger. Significant. Oliver. Love. The words swirl like confetti in my brain. If Mom hadn't dropped that "something significant" line, maybe we wouldn't have hit fast-forward on whatever this is.

"You laugh, but you'll see. This person holds the combination to your heart."

She's right. He does. "I hope everyone sees it that way. You know how Jac is about her brothers getting together with her friends. She's drawn the line in permanent ink and double-underlined it."

"Oh, sweetheart," Mom says with a warm sigh. "Forbidden fruit is never fully off the table when the heart is in the right place and the timing finally fits. Embrace your inner Eve and take a bite. Maybe it will rewrite the whole story."

"Thanks, Mom," I say and end the call before she can launch into a conversation about cosmic soul contracts. It's time for glam, and to get the wedding show on the road—or water as it may be.

GREENSEA GAZETTE

Islanders,

Ring-a-ling-ling! It's Wedding Day! And the rain gods are having their way. Have no fear: Thanks to your quick thinking and hard work, everyone will stay dry at the wedding except for our eyes as we witness this heartfelt union.

Miles has flown the best glam squad in Hollywood to our little island to spruce up the wedding party. Think Taylor Swift's glam. To be honest, I can hardly wait to see what they do with my green eyes.

We can at least say thank you to Mayor Nickerbottom for stopping all roadwork on island bike lanes. (Praise be for the wedding; they should've stopped that work a long time ago!) Don't come at me, bikers! We've been through this: Bike lanes to nowhere help no one. If the city committed to creating them across the entire island, it would be a different story.

Behold the swan boats that are filling Grays Bay adding to the wedding decor, and for your enjoyment. Thank you Johnny Nickel for the kind donation. All profits raised will benefit the Greensea Island School District, and boy, can they use it.

Greensea, you have outdone yourself! The yarn art on the downtown street signs is divine. If you haven't seen it, go check it out. The street sign poles are wrapped in blue or green and topped with a red pointed hat. GG loves it and doesn't care what the mayor says. Gnomes may be small, but they're mighty reminders that our voices still matter— even when the powers that be try to turn down our volume.

xoxo,

GG

CHAPTER SIXTEEN

OLIVER

Guests watch from the ferry deck as our limo bus pulls onto the ferry. Felicia's floral garlands decorate the railings around the boat with ribbons flapping in the wind. The rain has stopped—for the moment—but the clouds still hang low. So much for Jac's dream of exchanging vows against a magnificent sunset.

One of Miles's assistants—sunglasses and clipboard at the ready—directs the bus to the park near the elevator, where we leave Johnny to finish primping for his big moment, and go upstairs to the bridal party holding area—a curtained-off area on the main floor.

A hostess greets us at the top of the steps with a glass of champagne with an elderflower garnish—a Greensea Glow. I take a generous sip in the makeshift dressing room. Ferry booths are covered by curtains lining the area to give us privacy. Several full-length mirrors stand in different areas along with studio chairs ready for glam touch-ups. It's more like we're backstage at an awards show than on a boat getting ready for a wedding.

Mom, Dad, and Anne sit at one of the remaining booths.

"Don't you all look handsome." Mom rises to greet us, arms already stretched out for a hug.

"Mom! You're spilling on my pocket square!" Dave pulls away from the hug.

The curtains sway, and Tippy and Sylviane walk in, followed a moment later by Daisy. She floats in a dusty blue dress covered in lace flowers. Her long curls are pinned up with soft tendrils falling around her face, all topped off by a crown of wildflowers in a variety of colors.

A current runs between us as our eyes lock. I watch the corners of her mouth turn up and then quickly return to flat when Tippy taps her on the arm.

I chug my Greensea Glow and set the empty glass down on the table.

Miles runs in with a headset on, wiping sweat off his brow. "Ok, people! Ten minutes till we depart. Ten minutes, people!"

Makeup artists descend with a variety of brushes and powders looking us over and deciding what we need.

"All natural, please," Daisy reminds the makeup artist.

"Give it up! You're going to be on the sea with salt air hitting you. Let them do whatever they'd like," Tippy scoffs.

The curtain flutters, and Jac appears.

The room lets out a gasp.

Josh walks over and grabs her hands.

"You look gorgeous. A real life ferry-tale princess," he says.

And he's right. Jac is radiant in an unapologetic white silk slip dress. Her curls fall around her shoulders, held back by a beaded headband with a veil attached.

Miles runs up to her and snaps his fingers about his head. Two women appear with a lace train. They stand on either side of Jac and tie the train around her waist with a grosgrain ribbon bejeweled with a diamond floral buckle in the center.

"In all the weddings I've been to and managed, I've never seen anything like that, darling." Miles stands with his hands on his hips. "But it looks so stunning every bride should take notes," he insists.

The brother hug train continues and Dave takes a turn before it's mine. They share a quick laugh and my nerves flare up. I hate keeping things from Jac, but this will wait until after.

Jac hugs me and whispers in my ear, "I know."

My whole body goes cold. I pull away and scan her face. It's blank and showing no emotion.

"I was copied on all the wedding videos. When I didn't see your reenactment as part of the montage last night, I went back and looked while everyone was busy taking care of things because of the rain."

She takes a deep breath. "You two light up the screen." There's no intonation in her voice; she's not giving us her blessing.

I'm cemented to the floor. Not even a tidal wave could move me. I can't gauge her reaction.

"Jac, um, uh," I stammer as the ferry blasts its departure horn.

"Groomsmen, head upstairs," yells Miles.

"Just go," she says with a flick of her wrist.

And I do.

But my chest is on fire.

Shit. Shit. Shit.

I start toward the steps when the ferry lurches like someone stepped on the gas and then stopped short.

"Ahh!" Tippy screams. "Damn Captain Ferry McSwoony! That mascara wand just poked my eyeball!"

Champagne glasses clink. Something clatters in the main dining area.

"It's all okay. It's okay." Bell Meadowcroft's voice says in the distance.

Instinctively, I reach toward a table but bump Daisy's arm. Her skin's warm. She leans into me.

Daisy pulls her arm away as Jac yells, "Is anyone hurt? What just happened?"

"If I have to wear a patch for the wedding of the century..." Tippy's voice drifts off.

An assistant with a clipboard runs in and says, "Candelabras are down, but they're fixing them. No one worry!" She uses so much emphasis that even I start to worry.

Miles walks between Daisy and me.

"For the love of lipstick," he whisper-yells. "Get a hold of yourselves. Let Jac get married, have her first dance, I don't know. Let her throw her garter or something! Maybe even go on her honeymoon...and then you two can lock lips on land or wherever you'd like."

Holy crap. Are we that obvious? Does everyone know? I mouth, "*sorry,*" to Daisy and turn around and take a step toward the stairs, this time for real.

But the ferry thrusts forward and backward again and there's a sound like a giant can popping open. And then the entire ferry bumps into something. Daisy falters, and I reach for her waist, steady her, and pull my arms back quickly.

Sylviane falls off the stool where her makeup is being retouched. Josh runs over and helps her up. Something clatters in the dining area—again.

"What the hell?" Dave assumes a Spider-Man position, ready to catch anyone or anything.

"Nobody else move!" yells Miles, who's gone from wedding planner to emergency helper.

Assistants run in from behind the curtains in multiple directions. Someone with a blonde bob whispers in Miles's ear. He clears his throat.

"Everyone stay put. I'll go assess the situation." Miles charges away followed by a bevy of helpers.

Scanning the room, I see Jac. Dad's standing behind her with his hands on her shoulders. Mom and Anne are huddled together, whispering. Out of nowhere, Johnny appears with his hand over his eyes.

"Where's Jac? Is she okay?" he asks.

"We're all fine here. Only a little rattled," I say to Johnny who leans into whisper something in my ear.

"Things are off to a very literal rocky start. I don't want to upset Jac anymore. Between the rain, the ferry palaver, and you and Daisy, I'm afraid she may head for shore."

"Got it, man," I say. "And, um, I'm sorry."

"I know you are. Just keep it in your pants."

Shit. At least it wasn't ever out of my pants.

Miles gallops into us and whispers, "I believe the boat is fine. Captain McHotty hit a piling."

"That's a relief," I say.

"Well, I started with the good news. The bad news is McHottypants hit his head," says Miles.

"Holy hell! Is he okay?" asks Johnny.

"Oh, I'm certain he'll make a full recovery. But I've been informed that even if we don't go anywhere, which now we're not, we need to have a boat captain at the helm or we'll have to remove all the people."

"Bloody hell, we can't do that." Johnny unbuttons his tux and rubs his hands through his hair, causing a makeup artist to gasp.

"Mr. Nickel! Your hair! Don't mess it up!"

"We've got bigger things to worry about than my hair, darling."

Time to make up for my transgressions. I scan the guest list spreadsheet in my mind, thinking of every islander who might have a captain's license. There has to be somebody who can step in.

And then it hits me, I know just who to ask.

"What about Sam?" I ask.

"What about him?" asks Johnny.

"Isn't he a boat captain?"

"Bloody brilliant!" Johnny slaps my back, then runs to find Sam.

Mayor Nickerbottom arrives in a full tux and top hat, looking like he's ready to greet the groundhog.

"People, you need someone at the helm immediately, or I'm evacuating the boat. According to code 13.1.2, every marine vehicle must be manned by a licensed—and not unconscious—captain."

"We know." I try to stay calm. "Sam is a captain and will be at the wheel momentarily."

"Fantastic, but if he's at the wheel, who will marry the couple?" asks Mayor Nickerbottom. "According to Washington State law, all marriages must..."

"Okay. Okay. We understand," says Miles, quieting the mayor.

A gentle jingle comes up behind me, and I start when a hand touches my back.

"How can I help?" Daisy asks.

"Unless you're a chaplain in your spare time, you can't."

Daisy arches her eyebrows. "Are you joking?"

"No! There's no one to marry them! Instead of worrying about the rain, we should have been worrying about who was going to drive this boat responsibly. How the hell did the captain knock himself out?" My voice is louder than it should be.

Tippy swooshes by me. "I'll get the skinny on everything that's going on."

Daisy touches my shoulder. "I'm an ordained minister. I thought I told you I officiated Igor's wedding. I married couples at Burning Man last year."

Now that I think of it, she did mention something about that, but I thought it was the ashwagandha talking.

"And that's all aboveboard?" I can only imagine Burning Man offers crash courses on how to host group marriages.

"Yep, I'm a card-carrying ordained minister who can marry anyone with a marriage license."

Without thinking, I kiss her forehead.

"Are you kidding me, Oliver?" Jac yells from across the boat.

"No! No! It's not what you think!" Daisy runs to Jac and leaves me standing there with my heart dangling in the wind.

GREENSEA GAZETTE

Islanders,

The chairs toppled. A few people—none of my Fit Greenies, mind you—wobbled. But only the captain has been officially hobbled.

Turns out, good looks do not equate to steering skills. Captain McSwoony has crashed the wedding ferry. Okay, "crashed" might be a tad dramatic. He bumped a piling. But the metal-on-metal screech you heard was Hunter Sorenson's equipment grinding along the upper deck.

Our dreamy captain did manage to take himself out of commission by cutting his head on the wheel. The medic on board (Miles Marryright was truly prepared for everything, but a bummer we had to utilize his services) stitched up McClumsy and diagnosed him with a mild concussion. A little dramatic flair for the pre-ceremony festivities, perhaps? Regardless, I fully expect to see him at The

Reformation next week, working on his core. The captain must not go down with the ship.

Bell Meadowcroft and her team are already re-straightening tables with military precision. Thankfully, none of the candles had been lit. Toppled is inconvenient. Engulfed in flames? Less charming.

Felicia Higgins is reassembling flower vases like it's her personal relay event. And honestly, a little water on a tablecloth just makes the whole thing more authentically PNW-chic.

Someone give Violet VanWoosen a gold medal. Not only is she Greensea's hottest new baker, but her reflexes are next level. She saved the cake mid-lurch, and only a bit of icing touch-up was required. The vegan buttercream frosting lives on.

While there will be no cruise around the island (a tragedy for our wind-blown photo ops), the ferry will remain floating safely in Grays Bay. Maritime law says a captain must be present, and thanks to a last-minute switcheroo, we've got a new one at the helm.

So yes, the boat is staying. The guests are staying. And love —despite a few bumps and bruises—is still very much afloat.

xoxo,

GG

CHAPTER SEVENTEEN

DAISY

Jac's train flows behind her as she marches through the glam area and pushes the doors open to the bow of the boat.

"Jac! Wait! It's not what you think."

She stands at the green railing, looking every bit like Kate Winslet in *Titanic*, which is easier to focus on than the fact that my best friend is furious with me.

"What was the first thing I asked you not to do when I met you?"

I sigh. "Hook up with your brothers. But that's not what this is. This is something real, something big. I love the way he thinks of everything before I can think of anything. I love that..."

Jac cuts me off. "There were three people I asked you to keep off limits."

Even though the ferry is stationary, her veil blows in the wind. If she weren't so angry, the picture would be stunning.

"I know, and I'm sorry."

"I didn't want to lose either of you. You are my best friend, and he is my brother. I need both of you. When this doesn't work, I'll have to say goodbye to one of you, and blood is thicker than water."

Her face is filled with resolve. She's not questioning whether or not I like Oliver; she's telling me I can't.

"How do you know it won't work?" I ask like it's my last question before the bachelor gives me a rose or sends me home.

"Because you're opposites. You like sound baths, and he likes two-minute cold showers. He's corporate America, and you're the Boho Queen of the West Coast. But the worst part of this whole thing, Dais?"

Worse? There's more? I take a breath, the kind that burns a little on the way down. I dab the corner of my eye, hoping she doesn't notice the tear that's forming.

"You lied to me last night. I thought I knew you better."

Her words cut right through me.

"I'm sorry, Jac. I didn't mean to lie." I fuss with the flowers on my dress, anything to keep my hands busy.

I've hurt her, and arguing with her on her wedding day feels wrong, like laughing at a funeral. And beyond that, she's not just the bride. She's my best friend. The one who walked every messy mile with me from teenage chaos to something resembling adulthood.

If she's really asking me not to go down this road with Oliver, then I owe it to her to stop. As much as it tugs at my heart, it's easier to step back from something that's barely begun than risk blowing up the most important friendship I've ever had. Assuming she'll forgive me for lying to her.

"I'll let my feelings go. I won't act on anything. I promise. Now let me marry you—because I need this moment to be about you."

"You?" She makes fists with her hands like this is the last bit of bad luck she can't take.

"Yes. You don't have any other options. Sam has to captain the ferry now that McHotty or whatever his name is is out of commission."

To be honest, I'd be happy to slink off into the sunset, but the circumstances are forcing me front and center.

"Are you qualified to do this, or am I going to find out in a year that you were just licensed through some woo-woo church, and our marriage will only be legal on a reservation in Nevada?"

"No, I'm fully ordained."

Jac huffs and looks out at the bay. "Nothing is turning out like I dreamed. All these things keep going wrong."

"Yeah, well, perfect weddings don't guarantee perfect marriages. You know that better than most." My words resemble a steak knife when I was going for a butter knife, and I wish I could take them back. So I try again.

"This is a good thing. You're weathering your storms. Every obstacle the universe is throwing at you, you're figuring out. You don't need the outside stuff to be perfect when the inside stuff is."

Jac takes a deep breath. "Marry us, Daisy. I can keep a better eye on you if you're standing in front of me."

Great. Now I have to prove to my best friend that I'm honoring her word. I go to hug her, but realize I'll mess up our makeup and hair if I do.

"I love you, and I'm sorry I've added to the stress."

"I know you do. I'm glad you understand Oliver was a mistake." Jac turns to walk back inside.

A chill runs through my body, and I realize I have no other choice but to focus my energy elsewhere.

I catch a flurry of action as the wedding party backs away from the door, pretending they haven't been standing there straining to hear our conversation.

———

The sun deck is in full wedding triage mode. Things are buzzing. Teenagers brush water off the deck. A few guests are standing chairs upright as the rest of them hold umbrellas at the ready in case the rain returns.

At the top of the stairs, another assistant with an earpiece and—you guessed it—a clipboard greets me. She acknowledges my presence with a nod and pushes a button on her ear.

"Stand-in minister is here." She looks me up and down and hands me a sheet of paper. "Just read your lines and everything will be fine."

Yikes. At Burning Man, we exchanged very few words. And people were high on something in addition to life. For Jac's wedding, I'll want to say more.

"Follow me." She walks me along the railing to the bow of the sundeck covered by the canvas awning that the Needlers created.

Holy shit.

Somehow, in just a few short hours, they embroidered a stunning, enormous wedding sampler across the entire piece of canvas. In the center, a bride and groom are stitched inside a heart, with a ferry in one corner and a guitar in another. Beneath it all are Jac and Johnny's names and today's date—an instant heirloom. It's beautiful, no doubt. Though I do wonder where they'll put a sail-sized sampler. It's not exactly something you can frame and hang in the family room...or above the bed. But if anyone can figure out what to do with it, it's Jac and Johnny.

The thing that wows me the most as I stand here and look at the crowd is the collective love the community shows for each other. Even for me, an outsider.

I glance over the sheet of paper and make a few mental notes of places I can add some Daisy-isms.

And when I don't think I can handle one more moment of the love boat, the music cues up—an instrumental theme Johnny wrote for Jac to walk down the aisle. It's YoYo Ma with a Johnny flair. Think of every rom-com opening scene you've ever watched and then make it better. It's like they're all walking down the aisle on sunshine, hearts, and ferry dust as we blow in the sea breeze.

I avoid all eye contact with Oliver as he takes his place on the makeshift altar. Out of the corner of my eye, I can tell his head is facing mine. Knowing he's so close is enough to make my insides turn like a Mexican jumping bean.

As soon as Sylviane steps onto the altar, another processional begins. Everyone rises, and just when I think it's all too much, Jac appears on Tom's arm and walks down the aisle. There's something about the way she's holding her bouquet and smiling, that melts my heart. Happiness emanates from her as her aura glows with the sunshiniest yellow. Exactly the way I feel when I'm with Ollie.

Tom presents Jac to Johnny, and they stand in front of me holding hands with bated breath. I look at the script and drop it to the ground.

"Keep it legal," whispers Jac and I nod and continue.

"Welcome, family and ferry friends. We're gathered here today to celebrate something unique, maybe a tad unbelievable, but one hundred percent wonderful: two people who found each other accidentally and then chose each other on purpose. Even the universe sends its blessing on this union. In the rain, and when the boat lurches, and when it seems like people may be ignoring your wishes, the show must go on."

I take a breath and see Miles at the end of the aisle giving me hand signals to wrap it up.

"Jac and Johnny, he may be sushi and you may be peanut butter and jelly, but none of that matters because together you're magic."

They have eyes for no one else as they hold each other's hands.

"Now let's get to the good part. As we stand here, under an umbrella of love and community, I ask everyone to stand and hold your neighbor's hand, as we bless the union of this couple."

I turn to Jac who looks at me with softer eyes than earlier.

"Jac, do you take Johnny to be your husband, to love him, support him, help him with his crossword puzzles, and choose him again every single day?"

"I do," says Jac with a blinding white smile.

"Johnny, do you take Jac to be your wife, to love her, support her, stand by her side, and let her be the inspiration for your chart-topping music?"

He laughs and gazes into Jac's eyes. "I do."

"May I have the rings?" I ask no one in particular.

Miles bellows from the back, "Shit! The rings! Sam has them."

An assistant bolts. Laughter moves through the crowd. I bite the inside of my lip—thank goodness I'm not responsible for this.

An assistant sidles up the side aisle and hands me a silk pouch with the rings. I take them out and return the pouch.

Johnny and Jac stand in front of me—the air filled with love and a side of nerves.

"These rings are a circle of your love—unending and unbreakable. Let them be a symbol of your eternity together. Jac, your vows," I say.

"With this ring, I promise to love you through good chords and bad."

She places a ring on Johnny's finger.

"Johnny," I nod at him.

"With this ring, I promise to dance with you even when there's no music."

Johnny places the ring on Jac's finger.

"By the power vested in me by the state of Washington, I now pronounce you husband and wife. You may kiss your bride—and then let's celebrate before the ferry hits another piling."

And on cue, the ferry horn toots and the couple kisses to applause.

After the procession off the sundeck, Miles guides us down the steps, and the family converges in the holding area again before mingling with the rest of Greensea.

Oliver slides in next to me as soon as he sees an opportunity.

"That was beautiful, Dais. You were meant to be up there marrying Jac and Johnny."

"Thanks," I reply and take a step back, widening the space between us.

He takes a step toward me.

"Is everything okay?"

"Yeah, but—Ol." I close my eyes when I say the next part. "We can't do this." I turn around and walk away as a piece of my heart stays with him.

A full band, trumpets and all, plays jazz while people congregate in the reception space. A server hands me a ferry-tini, and someone else carries a tray with pretzel nuggets and popcorn.

The rest of the bridal party joins me at the reception just as there's a drum roll. Things are moving at a fast enough clip to make sure I don't have a second to think.

"Ladies and gentlemen, everyone put your hands together and welcome the spectacular new couple—Mr. and Mrs. Nickel!"

Jac's smile threatens her ears. She holds her bouquet in the air as she and Johnny sashay into the center of the dance floor to another round of applause.

We all take our seats and servers appear with trays of oysters on ice. The music quiets and Ollie clinks his glass as he stands to make a toast.

"To Jac and Johnny, who proved that you can find love when you least expect it."

He swallows a gulp of champagne and begins again. "Like when you find yourself driving down an island road in a borrowed VW bus and you look across at the driver and know that your heart made of spreadsheet cells would happily merge with something beautifully unpre-dictable—no formula required."

What is he doing?

Dozens of eyes stare at me and my flower crown. My cheeks burn but all I can do is look at the floor. His words tattoo themselves in my heart even as I try to shrug them off and hope they're written in washable ink. We cannot be a formula with a happy ending.

Thankfully, most people are none the wiser and clink their glasses in response and the new couple shares a kiss. Cutting ties to Oliver is going to be harder than I imagined. Can't he see he has to choose his family and not me?

A glass somewhere else in the room clinks and I take an opportunity to sneak out of the room while someone else makes another toast.

I hear Dave say, "Let her go, bro. Focus on your sister."

And that's all the confirmation I need.

I'm not sure where to hide. Ollie will be hot on my heels as soon as he has a moment. I go up the steps toward the sundeck but turn the opposite way and find myself in the wheelhouse—with Sam.

"How's it going down there?" he asks.

"Oh, fine. I mean, great. I just needed a break."

"Bloody hell, can't believe I'm up here missing my best bloke's wedding."

"But you saved the day. There wouldn't have been a wedding if you hadn't been able to take over," I remind him.

Sam smiles and nods his head. "Good point, Daisy."

"Mind if I take a minute up here?" I ask and plop down on a bench near the rear of the wheelhouse.

"My bridge is your bridge, Daisy Bennett!"

My phone pings with a text from Adam checking in to say that he can't wait to see me on the flight back to SFO tomorrow.

Shit. I promised Meredith I'd work at the store and it's an awkward time to ask the Shermans if I can stay longer.

"What are your plans after the wedding, Sam?" I ask with the glimmer of an idea germinating in my head.

"Funny you should ask, Daisy. I'm planning on running a yacht charter business around the islands here."

"You are?" I ask.

"Sure am. Fell in love with this area over the last year, and I'm going to helm summer cruises around here. Maybe spin up to Canada."

Bingo. "Any chance you have space for me to stay for a bit? I'll do all the cleaning and earn my keep."

"Well, Daisy, that sounds like a brilliant idea!"

I say a silent thank you to the universe for presenting me with more options and I text Adam back.

> Daisy: Staying in Greensea a little longer.
> I'll text you when I'm back in town.

"Thanks for letting me hang out with you," I say to Sam. "I guess I should go back."

"Anytime, Daisy," he winks while I linger at the door. "But would you do me a favor?"

"Sure! It's the least I can do!" I'm happy to have a job to keep me occupied. Then I won't be focusing on how the grey tux skims Oliver's body in all the right places. Or how it brings out the blue in his eyes.

"Bring me some food! All the courses!"

"Of course!" And I whisper, "Thank you."

Sam gifted me with the perfect reason to come and go from the reception. And a much needed distraction.

GREENSEA GAZETTE

Islanders,

If you were lucky enough to score an invite to the wedding of the season, congrats, you're still reveling in all the details. But for the rest of you...here's a little recap of the glorious day.

Bridesmaids were dressed in a collage of colors. Daisy Bennett—maid of honor turned guest officiant—wore a transcendent blue, while Sylviane DuPont radiated in rose, and I, Tippy Meadowcroft, insisted on representing the island in emerald green.

The groomsmen were dapper in pale grey suits with pocket squares to match their respective bridesmaid, although some may be regretting that idea today. Not all stories are fit to repeat.

You've seen Jac's resplendent dress all over the Internet and Johnny's midnight-blue velvet (yes! Even in July!) tux. Something only a rockstar could pull off.

Guests were greeted with a Greensea Glow—a glass of champagne with a sprig of elderflower. Although there was no sunset cruise as the bride and groom exchanged vows (don't come to us for a letter of recommendation, McSwoony), everything else went off without a hitch. After the ceremony, guests were treated to (or tortured by) tunes by the Alley Cat Junkies, the band you've seen busking all over the area. Trays of oysters from Sherman's Shellfish caught by Dave himself, whetted all of our appetites before we devoured a feast cooked by Hunter Sorenson. Each guest was treated to a filet of sustainably caught King salmon wrapped in parchment, garnished with dill, and served with Greensea-grown carrots, potatoes, and leeks. Hunter, you outdid yourself, and many of us would have had seconds if they were available.

After dinner, the new couple danced to old-school crooners. The father-daughter dance brought tears to our eyes when Jac and her dad, Tom, broke out in a choreographed little number. Tom, you're going to give Barb a run for her money on TikTok.

Oliver Sherman was the lucky recipient of the garter. Yes, slightly cringe that he caught his sister's garter. We hope he finds someone suitable who meets the family's stringent requirements soon. And Laura Prescott showed off her impressive Pilates moves when she managed to stay upright as she caught the bridal bouquet. If legend and lore bring a mate to Laura, that will be a tale to tell.

Violet's desserts did not disappoint, and in another viral moment, Jac got Johnny good when she smashed cake all over his rockstar profile.

The only minor hiccup (after the major ones) was the inability to bring the ferry to the dock. Swan boats were called in, and so began the tedious process of guests transferring into swans off the loading ramp and pedaling their way to shore. Did dresses get wet, and shoes come off? Absolutely, but we know most of you had no intention of wearing your wedding outfit again anyway.

If you ask me, all the unexpected twists simply made the wedding all the more special. For no one can replicate it. It had all the charm of Greensea that you've grown to love. Simply put, the wedding was a dream and will not be forgotten.

The happy couple will be off on their honeymoon to an undisclosed location (don't even try figuring it out, stalkers!) after a family brunch and send-off.

xoxo,

GG

CHAPTER EIGHTEEN

OLIVER

I spent most of the wedding trying to figure out where Daisy kept going. She'd float into the dining room, chat with a few people, and then disappear again. This happened at least a half dozen times. The last time she did it, I noticed her carrying a slice of wedding cake and followed her up to Sam on the bridge. Of course she's bringing him food while he's stuck up there, manning the boat. That's so Daisy, taking care of others.

And now I wait for most of the wedding guests to disembark the ferry via swan, at a glacial pace, as I twirl the mixer in my ferry-tini and wish things were ending differently. Pedaling off the ferry into the twilight with Daisy at my side—now that would be the frosting on the cake. Instead, I'm completing a mental risk assessment of going after Daisy.

"Can you believe this?" asks Mom, who finds me at the back of the line.

"I can't believe much of what's happened over the last

few days," I reply. Borrowed buses, stolen kisses, ferryboat crashes.

"I'm sure glad Jac and Johnny were on the first swan to shore," she says.

I nod. Me too. Jac's watchful gaze was getting tiresome. I was afraid to go to the bathroom without being followed.

"Come sit with me, Oliver. These heels are killing my feet."

Mom walks on her tiptoes to a quiet table in the corner of the boat.

"What's got you so pensive? Didn't you have fun at the wedding?" she asks.

I run my hands through my hair. "The wedding was great, Mom. It's nice to see Jac so happy."

"Ollie, stop with the greeting card lines. I know something's going on with you. I can tell from a mile away when things aren't right with one of my kids, and I'd think after all these years you'd quit pretending I can't."

I take a deep breath. "It's nothing."

"Oliver Franklin Sherman, I can tell from that sigh it's something. Spill it."

"I've kind of fallen for Daisy. Like head over heels. I'd buy a ticket to Burning Man and hang out in the desert for her."

Her eyes widen, and a smile blooms across her face. "You two would be the chef's kiss together. I've always thought you've had a spark."

"But what about the family rule?" I ask surprised by her easy approval.

"Oh goodness. That was meant to keep hormones in check. Not for real love."

"I don't think Jac sees it that way." I stare at my hand, rubbing my thumb over my knuckles.

"Jac is focused on her wedding. I don't know a bride alive who would want her brother hooking up with her maid of honor on her big day. That spells mess. But you and Daisy dating? That's a different story. And I think she'll see the light tomorrow morning."

My shoulders slump, remembering what Daisy said. "I don't think Daisy's willing to risk it."

"You don't know until you try, and I think it's worth giving it a go." Mom winks at me. "I'll take some of the heat from the family if there is any."

For the first time all night, I have a glimmer of hope.

Sam walks up to the table as his official business at the helm is done.

"Your turn on the swans," he says adding to my change in fortune.

"Do you know where Daisy is?" I ask, hoping she shared something on one of her visits to the bridge.

Sam looks at me, then Mom. "I probably shouldn't share this with you, but I have a good feeling about this whole thing."

Mom nods her head, encouraging him.

"She's staying on my boat," he says with a wink.

"Thanks," I say.

I link my arm in Mom's and offer some support as we walk downstairs to the loading ramp. Miles and his assistants seem to have a system in place helping guests into the boats. The wedding favor bags have made their way to shore and are being passed out as guests walk up the road. The entrepreneurial teenagers are taking guests to their cars on their pedal pub. And it looks like the golf department at Thin Pines Country Club has mobilized all their golf carts to help transport as well. When Greensea senses a story, we pull together and show up.

Mom takes the opportunity to go live on TikTok as I pedal her to shore on the swan boat, memorializing the snafu for all her viewers.

Walking over to Dad and a waiting golf cart, Mom takes my hand in hers.

"Go find her, Oliver. This is a chance you don't want to miss." She kisses my cheek and leaves me to walk over to the dock Sam's rented in Grays Bay.

It's not hard to find his yacht as it towers over the normal-sized boats in the marina. Sam's resembles a floating hotel. It belongs off the Amalfi coast toting rich billionaires around, and not hanging out in a marina on Greensea with fishing boats, ferries, and rowboats.

I walk up the plank to the main deck, which is covered in couches that wouldn't dare fit in my apartment. A large dining table—big enough to seat a dozen. A marble-topped bar. There's a big screen TV with a soccer game on.

As I venture further into the sea palace, I find a gold spiral staircase that leads down to four bedrooms. I'm straddling the line between lurker and romantic hero as I tiptoe around the boat looking for Daisy.

I peek into the bedrooms, each one decorated in pristine navy and white with walls paneled in shiny wood. No sign of Daisy in any of them. There's another smaller spiral staircase tucked at the end of the hallway that I follow down to a crew area with a large kitchen and dormstyle bedrooms.

Jeez. When Sam decided to buy a boat, he did not hold back.

I take the stairs back up to the rooftop and find a hot

tub and another sitting area. It's quiet up here with a light sea breeze.

And that's when I see the glow of candles and Daisy, her wildflower crown askew, sitting with a blanket on her lap. Like a Renaissance painting you'd find in a museum. The scent of incense wafts through the air, and I wonder if she's having a seance.

I clear my throat so I don't scare her.

"Ollie." She sits up straighter. "What are you doing here?"

"Heard you might be here, and I wanted to come by."

"You shouldn't have." She looks forward toward her candles.

"What are you doing up here?" I step closer to her.

She sighs, and says, "I'm cutting the cord between us."

"What?" My voice is louder than I anticipated, and I hear it echo through the harbor. "You're having a breakup ritual with me?"

"It's not a breakup if we were never officially together." She watches the flames instead of meeting my eyes.

"Still!" I blow out all the candles and sit down on the table in front of her.

"Oliver! You can't just come over here and take over my space."

"I'm not trying to take over, but I don't want you to sever us before I've even had a chance."

Daisy's lip trembles as she sits back on the couch and I sit next to her.

"I want to give us a chance," I whisper. I set my palm in her lap hoping she'll put her hand in mine, but she doesn't.

"How can we? Jac was pretty clear."

"I know she was, but with the wedding behind her, she'll think differently."

"You don't know that." She bites her lower lip—her nervous tell.

"But it's worth it to me to try to convince her. You're worth it to me."

Daisy wraps the blanket around her shoulders even tighter. "She's also upset because I lied when we were using the Magic 8 ball and she asked if there was someone in my life."

"Not a mortal sin. A white lie, that's it." I let out a laugh. "There's something here. And I'd think with all your beliefs, you'd realize that there's no denying what the universe is telling us is meant to be. We need to follow the signs, no matter what Jac says."

"It's not just Jac," Daisy replies. "The whole Sherman clan feels the same way. I heard Dave tell you to let me go."

I roll my eyes. Stupid brothers. "I talked to my mom earlier. She's given us her blessing."

Daisy looks at me like I've finally said the almost right thing.

"Really?" She raises her eyebrows with the first bit of hope I've seen.

"Yes, really."

I place my hand on Daisy's knee and lean in slowly for a kiss. The sea air disappears between us leaving nothing but the electricity around us. This is our first kiss that isn't hidden or stolen. It feels like destiny.

My whole body sings as her lips caress mine. Her flower crown tickles my forehead as she melts into me.

"My mom had another premonition," Daisy whispers between kisses.

"I'm afraid to hear."

"No, this time she said to take a bite of the forbidden fruit."

The image is more than I can handle and I pick Daisy up and carry her to one of the bedrooms.

"The universe just cracked open a new fairy tale," she says.

"Or a ferry tale," I correct as I lay her on the bed.

———

The house is filled to the brim with food and people. The table's loaded with every breakfast treat you can imagine. Piles of danishes and muffins. Egg casseroles, French toast. You name it, it's there. Mom must have stayed up all night making this feast.

All eyes are on us when Daisy and I walk into brunch holding hands. Enough pretending. I'm going to do this, and my family can take it or leave it.

"Well, well, well. What do we have here?" asks Dave.

This was either the worst idea I've ever had or the best. There's only one person who can tip the scales, and I'm holding my breath until she speaks.

Daisy clasps my hand a little tighter. All eyes turn to Jac, who puts down her plate and walks over to us at a turtle's pace. Is she going to smile? Are those tears in her eyes? I can't tell, but I realize I'm holding my breath waiting to see.

In what I think is a good sign, Jac grabs Daisy's hand.

"I'm so sorry to both of you." She looks between both of us. "I just couldn't think about anything but the wedding."

She takes a deep breath. "But I rewatched the video of the two of you hooking up..."

"What?" yells Josh. "Did you make a sex tape?"

Daisy turns three shades of red.

I give Josh a death stare. "Chill, no, we did not make a sex tape." I can't believe I'm standing in my parents' kitchen saying those words.

"I swear, it was just a reenactment. We only kissed," Daisy spouts out. "Well on the beach, we only kissed but...last night...."

I squeeze her hand. The rest of the story does not need to be told.

Jac continues. "There's something there. I should have seen it earlier. I practically forced you two together this week, always matching you up and having Ollie fly out to get you."

"Don't try to take credit for this." My smile creeps up. "We're together despite all of you."

"I'm sorry I lied," says Daisy.

"I think we can all agree that was hardly a lie," says Johnny. "No use crying over spilt tea."

"Dude, I think you mean milk," says Dave.

Johnny flicks his hand. "Whatever! Off we trot...time for a hug, ladies."

Daisy wraps her arms around Jac. Mom breaks the moment with a clap of her hands.

"I, for one, could not be happier about this union. More time with Daisy for any of the Shermans is a win!"

All the tension slips away and the regular laughter and chatter that fills these walls return.

Daisy and I take our seats, and Dad serves everyone mimosas.

"To bliss!" He raises his glass. We all follow, and I give Daisy's knee a squeeze underneath the table.

I take a second to look around the table. We've all found happiness. A couple of years ago, we were a ragtag group searching for something in different places. Josh was trying to flee Greensea but fell in love with Sylviane. Dave and Tippy turned a feuding relationship into a loving one. Jac met her true love right here in this room.

Now we're all smiles, finding our place in the world. Our table's growing and we're all the better for it. Everything's changing, but the room's still filled with the loud, loyal, and slightly chaotic love that only a Sherman family gathering can bring.

There's a honk in the driveway and Jac and Johnny exchange a look.

"Daisy," Jac says. "Come outside for a second."

Jac and Daisy run toward the door. I follow, just in case my sister's decided she's not into our relationship and she's having Daisy kidnapped.

Daisy stops in the doorway.

"Misty?" she asks.

And Jac nods. Daisy runs out the door to an all cleaned-up VW bus with blue-and-white gingham curtains and a dreamcatcher on the rearview mirror.

"Figured you needed a reliable ride while you're working on Greensea," says Jac. Daisy jumps with glee and claps her hands before wrapping Jac up in a bear hug.

"How am I ever going to thank you?" Daisy asks.

"Easy. Don't break my brother's heart." Jac winks.

GREENSEA GAZETTE

Islanders,

Did anyone on this island think all the Shermans would find suitable partners? It happened and we'll never know how. Barb and Tom can head off on their RV adventures knowing there's nothing but happiness brewing for each of their kids.

Somehow, even though the island is sleepy in its post-wedding bliss, an enterprising soul has turned the hero of the wedding into garden gnomes. When we woke this morning, all the swan boats were gnome-ified with perfect pointy red hats. There's no way the mayor can have a problem with a fleet of garden gnome swans bobbing in the sunlight, especially when the swans turned out to play such a pivotal role in the wedding events. This seems like less of a prank and more like a well fitting tribute.

The gnomes beg a larger question: Should the government exist to curb the will of the population? Of course not. It's here to provide order and stability to our island in the PNW.

Mayor Nickerbottom and the city council have lost the plot. They're chasing after ridiculous rules and nitpicking about lawn decor rather than letting people express themselves...hello! First Amendment anyone? If they'd just ignored the gnomes way back when, they wouldn't have become a thing. The city issued a challenge to residents, and you know how islanders and all the lawyers feel about a good battle.

Who decides what our island should wear? Stop acting like overbearing parents insisting their preschooler wear matching socks. The fact that they're matching isn't the point—it's that the kid picked them out. Sometimes things can exist that you don't find aesthetically pleasing, and that's okay.

The best foot forward isn't always the prettiest. Let's not be so quick to judge a book by its cover. There's always a story behind it. And sometimes the story involves gnomes in feather boas and sequined red hats. Just roll with it.

xoxo,

GG

AFTERWORD

DAISY

Citrus and sea salt wafts through the air as Ollie moves through the apartment above Cedar & Fern, getting ready to make the 7:05 ferry.

"Hey, I'm going to go in a little late tomorrow and I wanted to see if you'd join me for an excursion." Ollie leans down to give me a kiss.

"Sure. What for?" I ask.

He strokes my cheek.

"Nora Cunningham is going to take us to look at some houses."

"What?" I sit up in bed. "You're moving here?"

Ollie spends most nights on the island with only an occasional night in the city.

"I want to." He clears his throat. "Umm...hoping someday soon you'll move in with me."

My heart beats faster. The studio is small and better suited for one. And the bell on the door signaling customers gets to be a little bit much especially on

Saturday mornings when people are coming in for their baked goods. But it's a place I can call home on Greensea —because Tom Sherman is giving me a steep discount on the rent. I sigh. I can't afford to live anywhere else.

Ollie stops buttoning his shirt and sits down next to me on the bed. "I know you're creating an Ollie-sized spreadsheet in your mind, but I've heard the gift economy is pretty vibrant and I bet we can work something out." He winks.

I want to grab him and roll around in the sheets. "I have a few ideas of things that might make great gifts," I tease. "I'd love to help you look for places, but until I have a better handle on my financial situation, I'm going to keep this place," I say, realizing it's the most un-Daisy statement I've ever made.

Ollie's white teeth glimmer in the early morning rays of sun. "I respect that and we'll take all the baby steps you need. I love you, Daisy Lou."

I roll my eyes but my insides are bubbling like a bottle of champagne. "You promised you wouldn't use my middle name anymore!"

"See you at tonight."

Outside, the gulls call to each other, and the breeze carries in a little more salt than usual—like the sea's blessing whatever this next step might be. We really have come a long way. Mr. Spreadsheet is ready to leap before he looks and I've found that being practical isn't all bad.

———

Every moment I spend at Greensea Gems reminds me I have found my new home on Greensea. The gems, the energy. It all speaks to my soul. Any time I question my decision, the universe sends a gentle nudge. A misplaced gem sharing the energy I need. A feather finding its way into the store. A penny on the ground. And the best sign of all? Meredith decided to stay and help her sister out, and I'm taking over Greensea Gems full-time. We're putting together a contract that will allow me to work toward full ownership. The perfect example of practical and woo-woo hints from the universe.

The bell rings, signaling customers.

"Hi! Welcome to Greensea Gems!" I say as a young couple walks in.

They both nod and look at the displays.

"Can I help you with anything?" I ask.

The guy looks at me, "Actually, yes. Can you tell us what time the 2:20 ferry leaves?"

That can't be a real question. Am I on *Candid Camera: Ferry Edition*?

"Umm...I'm new here, but I would assume it leaves at 2:20. Have you heard something different?"

"I wasn't sure if that was the time you boarded, the time it arrived, or the time it left."

"Huh, I guess I never thought that there were other options. But it's the time the ferry departs."

"Anywhere else we should visit while we're here?" he asks.

"Everywhere. Greensea is dreamy. Be sure to grab a cinnamon roll at Apollo. They're delectable. Codmother's has the best fish and chips out there. Oh, and Between the Covers has all the latest and greatest books."

"For someone new here, you seem to know a lot about Greensea and are overly enthusiastic about this island," he says as I catch a hint of disbelief.

"It's my energy vortex."

"Oh! Mine's Sedona," says the woman who's holding an aquamarine gem to the light.

"I love it there too." Igor gave me a list of places to visit when I went. "All that red rock. The energy twirls around you."

The guy looks between us like we're crazy and moves toward the door.

"Enjoy your stay in the vortex!" I say as they leave.

The bell rings again, and a sweaty Ollie appears turning the sign on the door to closed.

"How was your run?" I ask as he reaches over the counter for a kiss.

"Good, but have you checked your texts?"

"No." I pick up my phone from the counter.

Jac: Family meeting 6pm. Don't be late.

"That's ominous don't you think?" He runs his hand through his hair.

Jac and Johnny have been gone for a month, traveling around New Zealand.

"Not really. I'm sure they just want to tell us about their trip."

Ollie shrugs. "Has your mom said anything?"

"No, like a sign?"

"Yeah. She hasn't said anything bad was going to happen, has she?"

"Nope. I'm sure this is nothing."

———

After I rearrange the gems at the stop to balance their energy and Ollie takes a quick shower, we finally arrive at the Sherman house.

When we walk in, Tippy, Dave, Josh, Sylviane, and Jac are seated at the table. Dave's fiddling with the laptop, trying to pull Barb and Tom up on a video call, and Johnny's bringing Jac water.

Jac rolls her eyes and Johnny stands behind her. Dave, Josh, and Ollie exchange brotherly glances.

"Spill it, Jac. What's going on?" asks Dave.

Jac takes a deep breath, but Johnny jumps in. "Your sister is pregnant." His voice is all business and no joy.

"Is this a good thing?" I ask.

Jac giggles. "It is! Johnny is just freaked out! He won't let me do anything on my own!"

"The first trimester is tenuous..." Johnny begins, but we don't listen and all jump up to hug our girl.

"Careful! Careful!" Johnny yells.

And just like that the Sherman chaos resets itself around something new—a bundle of nothing but joy.

GREENSEA GAZETTE

Islanders,

Well, the cat's out of the bag! Nothing stays secret for long on Greensea. You all should know that by now. Time to trade the garden gnomes for storks! Jac and Johnny are expecting! Yes, stay tuned for the next generation of Sherman goodness. What happens when you mix old-school island royalty with a world-famous pop star? I guess only time will tell.

Best of luck to Oliver Sherman as the no longer eligible bachelor looks to re-establish his roots on Greensea. We hear he's looking at cozy cottages with perfect golden hour views and lots of Feng Shui—sounds like he's manifesting a forever kind of vibe.

Sam Neville and his crew have been sailing around the Puget Sound. He's looking for a few new crew members to help around the boat. If you're a bosun, steward, cook, or have at least watched endless episodes of Below Deck, *this could be for you. Turnover seems to be quick on the high seas. The city council approved the bid for Tide Together to call Greensea home. Rumor has it he'll be offering discounts to islanders to enjoy a cruise to nearby destinations. Good luck, Sam! We're so glad you're getting settled on Greensea.*

With the never-ending budget crisis dragging on at the state level, there are whispers about cuts that will have an impact on Greensea and the vessels that tie it to the mainland. Word around the harbor is that Mayor Nickerbottom is working on a plan. We're all holding our breath...

We hear there's a resurgence in dating app use on the island—for all ages. That tea's still steeping, but more to come.

xoxo,

GG

LET'S STAY IN TOUCH!

AN EXCERPT FROM THE HOUSEWIVES OF GREENSEA ISLAND

Meet the Housewives

Laura Prescott - I wear the pants at home and in the courtroom.

Amanda Willows - I'm the manager of minions and CEO of cuddles.

Kitty Reynolds - I like to dance like no one's watching.

Nora Cunningham - I hold the keys to fulfilling your dreams.

LAURA PRESCOTT

The clock says 7:16 a.m. The sun's barely above the horizon. My high-rise pants are already pulling my underwear up my butt. The breakfast burritos are getting cold. And I've had to shout upstairs seven times to get everyone out of bed.

The only thing pushing me forward during this morning's school rush is the thought of an overpriced drink at Troll Coffee House. But first I need to get these kids on their merry way. I've made it a habit to pack lunches filled with love notes and the recommended daily allowance of fruits and veggies chopped in creative shapes. Today I'm slicing an apple, using a tiny heart-shaped cookie cutter to cut out the center, and filling it with a piece of melon cut in the same shape. I'm hoping some child will go home and tell their parents what a great mom the Prescott kids have. That would absolve me from a multitude of other sins, like when I packed Doritos for a snack one day five years ago.

Jo and Meg run down four minutes late at 7:32. Meg packs her bag and grabs her breakfast to eat in the car on the way to school. Jo drops the burrito in the garbage, opens the pantry, and snags a handful of Oreos instead. A tiny part of me hopes the crumbs get stuck in between her teeth. It'll serve her right.

"Thanks, Ma," says Meg, kissing me on the cheek.

Jo grunts and walks out, obviously still upset about our argument last night. But they're off to school and now it's just George and me.

"Ready?" I take note that he's fully dressed and has on two matching shoes.

"Yeppers, Mama-roni!" George walks over to me with his arms up. I give him a quick smell check. Score one for the soap and one for George for actually using it.

"What's with the hair?" It's parted down the side and slicked back with some substance that seems to have left a residue.

"It's Dress Like Your Role Model Day and I'm dressed like the kid from *Home Alone*."

Of course he is, and I don't even care that he should have a better role model because he took it upon himself to remember what day it was. I'm convinced the school's mission is to keep me on my toes—or drive me mad—by inventing dress-up days I'm destined to forget.

"Grab your stuff and hop into Betty White. I'll be right there." I take my papers from the counter, toss them in my satchel, and head out to the overpriced Tesla Phil gave me before he told me he didn't love me anymore.

"Remember, George, Blake's mom is taking you to soccer practice and I'll pick you up."

"Got it!" Of all the Prescott kids, he's the most good natured in the morning.

Greensea Elementary is only a four-minute drive from the house, and if I time it correctly, I won't have to wait too long in the drop-off line. Which is exactly what I've accomplished today.

Georgie opens the door and gets out.

"Family rules, Georgie?" I yell, hoping they're ingrained in his brain.

"Listen to adults and don't be a d*&k!"

The door closes before I can remind him that's not exactly our family rule. But kid number three has a more mature vocabulary than I planned on. And of course Amanda Willows drives by with her window down, wagging her finger at me.

Betty White's almost on autopilot driving me toward the coffee I desperately need before I go to the office to mediate island residents' squabbles—which are as annoying as my teenage daughters' bickering.

I pull up to The Troll House, with a rounded brown door made of slabs, a green sloped roof, and a water wheel on one side. Objectively the cutest coffee spot in the state of Washington. There's a window next to the front door that you can use to place your order from your car.

The window opens and a little lady with short salt-and-pepper hair peers out. "What can I get ya?" Vera asks.

I'm always surprised she doesn't recognize the car, and hence my order, but maybe Vera doesn't pay that much attention.

"I'll have a triple-caff oat milk vanilla latte, please."

"Sorry, sweets. No goat's milk anymore." Vera pushes up her glasses and taps her pen on the pad of paper she uses to take down the orders. She's old school and a welcome improvement after the summer help has gone back to school.

"Oh, no, I said oat milk." Maybe Vera's hearing is going with her memory.

"Don't carry that. How 'bout some almond milk?"

"I've been ordering the same thing here every morning for ages, and nobody has ever said anything about not having oat milk."

"That's because I thought you were ordering goat's milk and we had it until yesterday when the mayor, who has to stick his nose in everyone's business, found out and made us throw it out. Apparently it's not 'legal'"—Vera uses air quotes—"to sell unpasteurized goat's milk."

I gulp. I've been drinking raw goat's milk all this time? Gross. I vomit in my mouth.

"I think I'll skip my drink today."

Vera shrugs and I roll up the window and pull away. Apollo will have to do.

My phone pings as I drive. On a normal day, I'd be at my desk right now, and I'm sure Becky is wondering where I am.

I pull up in front of Apollo and grab my purse. The sweet smell of cinnamon rolls greets me on the sidewalk, but since I have a deposition and can't get to Pilates today, I'll skip the extra calories.

The line's only about three deep, allowing me to catch up on my emails while I wait. I glance at the screen— there's an icon with a man's name next to it I can't read without my readers. There's no end to the way scammers will try to get ahold of you nowadays. I swipe it away and another one appears. What the heck! I swipe again and another one appears. I try to click my phone off but a text from Nora comes through first.

Nora: Well, well, well! Nice entrance to the dating world!

What is she talking about? Shit. She must mean Jo. Didn't she delete her profile like I asked her to last night?

Laura: Ugh. Sorry. It's the "in" thing for 18-year-olds to do. Thanks for letting me know Jo's profile is still up there.

Nora: No! Not Jo! Yours!

What. In. The. Actual....

"May I take your order?" asks the woman behind the counter.

"Um, yes. Sorry. Just a sec. Do you have o-a-t milk?" I will not risk another milk mix up.

The woman squints her eyes. "Yes, we have oat milk." She enunciates each syllable.

"Thank goodness. May I have a triple-caff vanilla latte with oat milk?"

She nods, writes my order on the cup, and rings it up.

I pick up my phone again and sit on the stool in the window while I wait. Three more notifications with names have popped up. I swipe on the most recent and it takes me to a message from **Herb Rutherford**—*International banker looking to invest in you*—that says, *I'll wrangle your pussy cats anytime you need help.*

I slam my phone on the bar harder than I mean to. Deep breaths. I pick my phone back up, click on Bumble, and search for my name.

Laura Prescott—*Frisky cat herder looking for a good time.*

I'm afraid my eyeballs might actually pop out of their sockets or I might combust.

There's a picture of me sitting on an enormous piece of driftwood at golden hour. I remember that moment. We were all on the beach together. I'm laughing at something George is saying. My hair's swinging in the breeze.

It's a good picture, and I'd post it anywhere, but I don't want it on a dating app. I don't want anything on a dating app!

I turn my phone over like if I can't see the screen, my profile will disappear.

Not many people have access to that picture—to be exact, only the kids and I have that picture on our camera rolls. And those words...I've compared parenting to cat herding. Clearly, someone pays more attention to what I say than I thought.

I call Jo at school. She doesn't answer, so I call back.

"Mom?" she whispers. "Is everything okay?"

"No!" I yell just as the cappuccino maker stops making steamed milk.

"I'm in physics," she whispers again.

"I don't care what class you're in! Did you put me on Bumble?" The older guy in the booth turns and looks at me. The barista I gave my order to smirks.

"Yep! Figured you must have been curious about it, since you were snooping around on it yesterday."

I was curious. Sue me. But I was not ready to get on the site.

"I just wanted to support you," she says. I swear I hear her lips turn up as she says it.

Before I can yell bullshit, my phone rings with another call. I pull the screen away from my face—it's Greensea Elementary. Shit.

"I've got to go." I hang up on Jo and take the other call.

"Mrs. Prescott?" says a female voice on the other end.

"Ms. Prescott," I correct her. I can't fathom why it matters to me now, but my compulsion to correct people is overwhelming.

"I'm sorry, ma'am. Principal Atkins asked me to call you."

I can't focus on her words. I put my head down on the counter. All I can do is wish I had some magic ferry dust to rewind time and make this morning disappear.

AMANDA WILLOWS

As soon as I start the car, my phone pings with directions, predicting it'll take eight minutes to reach Greensea Elementary. It's both impressive and unsettling how often my phone knows I'm headed to school—nine times out of ten, it's spot on. The directions from my phone are more than unnecessary, as I could make the drive—left turn, stop sign, right turn, and then straight ahead on the left—with my eyes closed.

Thomas's last words before he left for work echo as I pass each familiar landmark: Greensea Goat, Thin Pines. "Cleo's nine now. You know you're not getting paid to volunteer. There are other parents who can pitch in and help. Maybe it's time to start picking up some shifts at the clinic."

I haven't told him that just the other day, the mailman tracked me down at school with a package that needed a signature. Thomas is a broken record scratching his complaints at 33 RPM, and it's giving me indigestion. I will go back to work sometime. I will. Cleo's success is my only priority right now. And let's be real: I've seen the work of the other parents. Last year, someone sent in an empty tampon box for the Celebration of Platonic Friendships—a.k.a. Valentine's Day, but we're not allowed to say that. That fiasco required an impromptu lesson on feminine hygiene, leaving seven-year-old Jeannie Frank waking up at 2 a.m. convinced she was about to bleed to death.

Luckily, as the leader of the Greensea Girl Scout troop, I had access to enough boxes to save the day. Honestly, there's no question I'm the most qualified parent to take charge at Greensea Elementary. And no matter how much Thomas complains, I have to be there today, because it's Role Model Day—an early fall dress-up day formerly known as Halloween. Cleo's dressed as Greta Thunberg, and I'm dressed as Amelia Earhart. An easy costume that won't get in the way while I hand out the locally produced organic fruit leathers at snack time.

As I pull up into "my" visitor's parking spot, Laura Prescott's walking out the front door of the school. Her lips are moving a mile a minute but I don't see her phone or AirPods of any sort.

I throw the car in park and get out. "Talking to yourself, Laura?" I ask, pushing the button on my key fob to open the minivan door. "Can't find anyone to chat with on Bumble?"

She scrunches up her face. I have a habit of making snarky remarks toward people, especially those who don't frequently volunteer time or money. It's like I have an invisible hierarchy based on people's participation in events I care about.

She rolls her eyes and moves a tube of something around in her hands. Her fingers don't quite cover the lettering. "KY Jelly?" She tries to stick it in the pocket of her blazer but the words "personal lubricant" stick out. "What on earth are you doing walking out of an elementary school with sex lube?"

"Calm down, Amanda." She tries to bend the tube into her pocket. "It's not a big deal. Georgie thought it was hair gel. Just picking it up so it doesn't cause any more trouble."

What use does she have for lube? Her husband left her for greener pastures to be a traveling doctor. "Interesting product for a single mother of three!" I give her a friendly wink.

She finally throws it in her purse. "Georgie found it in the back of a cabinet. It's probably expired."

"Expired sex gel...even better."

"I'm late. I have to get to work."

I swear she emphasizes the word *work*. "As do I!" I chirp with a smile and grab the box of fruit leathers.

Laura opens her car door and looks at me. "Oh, that's great! Are you finally on the payroll here?"

She doesn't wait for a response. Her white Tesla purrs as she backs out of her parking spot.

It's barely 9 a.m. and I've had two too many conversations about payrolls. My stomach gurgles. I swallow a burp. I set the box down on the sidewalk and straighten the flight goggles that feel like they're strangling me.

"Morning, Amanda!" Patricia buzzes me in the front door of the school. I grab my badge out of the drawer at the front desk.

"Who are you dressed as, Patricia?" She's wearing an oversized grey knit poncho over a black shirt.

"Martha Stewart when she left prison!"

Reason no. 17 they need me at this school! "Are you telling the children you're dressed as an inmate?"

She laughs. "Of course they don't know that! The double entendre makes this costume so great!"

Great? This island has lost its mind. I need to get into the classroom. The fate of the future is in my hands.

"I'm going to hand out the treats." I escape to the hallway.

I love walking through the school. The smell of glue wafts through the corridors. Little voices bellow out of classrooms. Kids barely taller than my knees push past me as I walk to the first room.

"Hi, Mrs. Harris!" I hand her the bundle I counted and labeled for her class.

"Thank you, dear! Sure hope these taste more like fruit than leather." She takes them to her desk.

So do I. Ash and Vic Willard at Fork & Stable worked so hard to create these, puréeing, cooking, and then dehydrating their apples so we could have enough for every child. We need this to be a win. The PTO spent a disproportionate amount of our budget on this new snack creation, but it was the only way to ensure there wouldn't be any complaints and we could meet all the dietary and allergen restrictions.

My stomach grumbles—again. I grab one of the extra treats and take a bite. It's chewy and sticky. I'm worried the crown may pop off of my molar. Gosh, I hope we don't lose any teeth today! But I'm starved, so I finish it regardless of any potential tooth loss.

Behind me, I hear a little voice declare fruit isn't a treat. Someone else asks if it's a dog treat or a people treat. Great. My pricey idea isn't a grand slam.

I hand the rest out quickly while stifling a burp. What's wrong with me? I throw the box down in the hallway and run into the miniature bathroom. It's one of those with the toilet six inches off the ground so the little kids can reach it. I drop to the floor, twist the goggles to the back of my neck, hold my head over the kiddie-sized bowl, and throw up.

Did I just spontaneously throw up from the fruit? Shit. What if all the kids get sick too? I gag again. No, it can't be that. If it was the fruit, there'd be a bunch of munchkins getting sick in here with me. Must be something else. My stomach's been off since Thomas lodged his complaints this morning.

I stumble out of the stall and Miss Kitty, Cleo's dance teacher, is washing her hands at a miniature sink.

She catches my eye in the mirror and raises her eyebrows. "You feeling okay, Mrs. Willows?"

"Yes." I shake my head a little too vigorously. "Yes. Yes. What are you doing here?"

"A special dance class for PE classes today."

She looks me up and down and rifles through her bag, taking out a packet of Saltines. "These should do the trick for the, ahem, stomach flu."

KITTY REYNOLDS

Amanda Willows is pregnant. As a lifelong dancer and ballet teacher, I've studied the body in its many forms. I've observed friends and students go through all the stages of pregnancy. I know all the signs. When you're in tune with the body, one notices even the slightest change. Even without the sound of Amanda throwing up, I could have guessed she was pregnant by noticing the shifts in her figure.

Amanda leans down to the miniature sink, splashes her face with cold water, and takes a bite of the cracker, making a retching noise as she swallows.

"A little too much to drink at Wine Down last night?" I ask, knowing full well that's not the case.

"Certainly not!" She unzips her leather flight jacket and fans herself with a paper towel. "I must have a bug."

"Go home and get some rest. They'll survive without you today." The dark circles under her eyes are not from the ridiculous flight goggles she's wearing.

She takes a deep breath. "You're right. I am exhausted." She yawns. "Thanks for the crackers, Miss Kitty.

And, um, let's keep all of this," she moves her hands around in a circle, "between us."

I nod, and Amanda walks out of the bathroom. I look in the mirror and wet my fingertips to slick the few flyaways back into my ballet bun and tuck another secret into my metaphorical tutu.

The Greensea Mommies don't understand me. I'm an enigma—a forty-five-year-old woman without kids. They count me out, if they see me at all. But my invisibility gives me power and has crowned me the keeper of secrets from pregnancies to lice—because you can't hide much in a leotard and a slicked back bun.

As I open the door back out into the school hallway, little arms wrap around my legs. "I wuv you, Miss Kitty," says a pigtailed little munchkin. I stroke her head and tell her I love her too. I'm everyone's favorite Miss Kitty. I'm the first place my old students stop when they return from college and the last goodbye on the way to the ferry.

I hand in my visitor's badge at the office. Patricia barely nods as I stroll out the door and start the walk home.

The sun's reaching just above the treetops, scattering rays along the road. The sound of the breeze and chirping birds is welcome after a morning filled with the familiar sounds of elementary school—high-pitched voices vying for attention, bells dinging, and sneakers squeaking.

I walk everywhere I can. It's a habit I've saved from living in New York City and brought to Greensea. Hills dapple my walk from school, and there's no sidewalk until Main Street, but it's invigorating—the best way to keep my body leotard-friendly. I've traded city sidewalks for country lanes, but the feeling is still the same.

Our three-story, slim, modern mecca rises above the

tree line in Grays Bay. As I turn the corner, I see the lights twinkling on the third floor and notice Kit's car in the driveway.

We're a couple made in heaven—Kit and Kitty. We fell in love one night in a darkly lit bar near Juilliard, as we laughed about our names. I was almost thirty, ready to leave behind the grind of waitressing between shows and enduring awkward dinners with creepy men just to afford a decent meal. He was forty-five, divorced, and navigating life with teenagers. We started out long-distance, while he traveled to New York for work. Eventually, I made the leap and moved to Greensea, where I opened my dance studio. The rest, as they say, is history.

"Hi, love," Kit meows as I walk up the stairs to our top-floor living area. "How was school?"

"Oh, you know. The same as usual. Crawling with moms hovering over their kids." Don't get me wrong, I adore the children. I've spent most of my adult life teaching them. I wipe away tears. Fix hair. Tie shoes. But I don't want to tuck them in every night. Two things can be true at once.

I walk over and sit at the table. Kit brings me a bowl of yogurt topped with berries and granola. His second act in life as a dance teacher—something his finance bros never imagined—affords him freedom in his schedule and a flexibility I adore.

"We have a private lesson tonight. A first date," I say.

"Oh?" He kisses the top of my head.

"Yes, she said she wants us to pull out all the stops."

Kit raises his eyebrows.

"I'm going to head to the studio in a bit to set up. Join me later around six?"

Kit has rhythm and is the perfect partner in the

studio. The way he moves his hips—divine. He's a natural. A two-step here and a shuffle-ball-step there. I swoon every time he hits the dance floor.

"Wouldn't miss it," he says and rubs my shoulder.

I adore my life. I can go to sleep when I want. Wake up when I want. Kit dotes on me, bringing me flowers, a piece of dark chocolate he finds at the market, a velvet ribbon for my hair. I'm his treasure and he reminds me of it every minute he can. Kit's two kids, all grown up now, live in the city and visit often. I'm their Mama Deux. I've got everything I want, and the freedom to enjoy it all. People who don't understand are just jealous.

I have a plan for tonight's private lesson that I'm anxious to put into action. My studio, a renovated boat repair shop, is a seven-minute walk from the house, just behind The Old Owl—everyone's favorite local pub. It's big and airy. Rustic and perfect. A barre and mirror line one side of the room opposite the floor-to-ceiling windows. The rest of the space is open. The only modern touch is the top-tier stereo system.

Today I pull the long curtains in front of the windows. The exposed brick walls offer their own ambiance. I gather the rarely used candelabras and fill them with vanilla-scented votives. I rummage through the prop closet, grabbing all the masks we used for the Mardi Gras ball. I take the whip and the handcuffs from my private supply of props and hang them across the pillar in the center of the room. I scatter silk red roses across the floor and uplight the curtains with deep red lights. It's dark and seductive. The perfect vibe for our sultry tango lesson.

Kit walks in just before six. "You've outdone yourself, love." He's dressed in his black dance pants and a white shirt unbuttoned halfway to his navel. His hair is slicked back and his mustache turns up at the ends. He gives me a hug and we sashay across the room.

A breeze announces Nora's arrival. She's been one of my best customers, lining up early in the morning (I'm old school even with in-person registration) to register one of her sons for classes each fall. Roger was my star student and one reason I'm so willing to pull out all the stops for Nora and her date this evening.

Nora stuns in a pale pink mid-length dress and nude heels. Her blond hair hangs down around her shoulders in curls. She steps into the studio and looks around with her mouth open. Jackpot. She's speechless.

She takes another step further into the room and says, "Oh. My. God. I wanted *Dirty Dancing* with campy vibes and the lift at the end, not *Fifty Shades!*"

Shit. I take out my phone and re-read her text.

> Nora: think dirty dancing - a sexy and passionate first date

I never once thought about that cringey old movie.

"Nora, you said *sexy and passionate*," I remind her.

"Like *Dirty Dancing*."

"But, my dear, you didn't capitalize the letter 'D' in either word, so I didn't know you were referring to the movie."

Nora plays with her curls. "No time to do anything about it now. Think you can shove the whips and the handcuffs in the closet before he arrives?"

As if on cue, the door opens. Nora turns around and drops her beaded clutch on the ground. I hear Kit behind us, taking down the props.

"What are YOU doing here?" She rubs her hands down her pink dress as if she's trying to iron it.

Well, well, well. Tongues will wag after this dance lesson.

"I believe you asked me out on a date," says a deep voice.

Oh, Nora...the lowercase D is the least of your problems.

NORA CUNNINGHAM

Oh. My. Gosh. Why is he here? I look around the room for any kind of exit. Where's the fire door? Is that an earthquake I feel? A tremor? Please, let the ground open up and swallow me whole. Shit. Shit. Shit. Now I'm stuck in the dance studio on a date with my friend's kind-of-recent ex. A cat's got my tongue. An elephant's on my chest.

"Nora, you asked me out on this date, didn't you?" the deep voice asks.

"I asked GreenseaPhil123 out, not Phil Prescott." I grab my hair with both my hands.

"I'm not Phil Prescott, Nora. Surely you know that."

Right, right. Semantics. His last name is Young. Even so, it wasn't part of his profile.

I exhale, fighting against my Spanx. How could I be this stupid?

"Your photo was blurry. I could hardly make out the figure walking on the beach. I thought you were some random islander I just hadn't met." I make a mental note to check the prescription for my readers.

"Are there any random islanders you haven't met?" asks Kitty. I glare at her, urging her to pipe down.

But she's right. There aren't many islanders I don't know. I'm the top realtor on the island. Islanders are my business. But that still doesn't explain this situation. I should not be on a date with Laura Prescott's baby daddy. This is going to have to be put in the vault and thrown overboard on my next ferry ride.

I'm frozen in the middle of the dance floor even though my brain's moving at a mile a minute. "But wait a second, you knew it was me and still came?" Did he forget that Laura and I are friends? Did he forget Roger took Jo, his daughter, to prom?

"I realized Norakeystogreensea was you." He smiles with his entire face, showing off his most charming bedside manner. "The idea of a—let's see, how did you say it? 'A night moving to our own beat' enticed GreenseaPhil 1 2 3." His voice is as smooth as chocolate.

I pick up my clutch and walk toward the door. "Sorry to waste your time, Phil."

"You can't just leave," says Kitty, an octave higher than normal. "You hired us."

"Whatever." I wave her off. "I'll still pay for the lesson." There are fewer consequences if I pay and leave than if I pay and stay.

"Stay," says Phil.

He walks toward me. He's wearing tailored black dress pants that hug his legs—he hasn't given up running since the divorce—and a crisp white button-down shirt. He has his tweed sports coat casually draped over his shoulder. He reaches his other hand toward mine but I retreat to the door like his hand's on fire.

"A little dance won't harm anyone." His long dark

lashes pop against his pale brown skin. I shake my head to get rid of the visions of his eyelashes waltzing across my cheek. Damn, what is wrong with me? I shouldn't be feeling this desperate.

A gentle strum of a guitar rings out as Kit ignores my protests and cues up the music. Kitty struts over like she's walking on water. "Let's do this."

She takes the bag out of my hand and sets it on the table near the door. She walks—more like pushes—me toward Phil and takes my left hand and puts it in his right hand. Kitty places my right hand on Phil's shoulder and his left hand on my waist. Against my better judgment, I shiver.

"Kitty, are you trying to save money by keeping the thermostat so low?"

I should have brought a sweater instead of trying to show off my sexy arms from all my Pilates workouts at The Reformation, the old church that's come back to life as a Pilates studio. But let's be honest, the quiver was not from the temperature in the room. Every nerve ending in my body is bound and determined to betray me.

"Follow our lead," says Kitty. I watch her reflection in the mirror as she sashays toward Kit. They assume the same position she's placed us in and begin to dance with their hips.

"F-o-r-w-a-r-d, f-o-r-w-a-r-d, forward, forward," Kit croons. "And again."

The warmth from Phil's hand creeps across my entire body. I'm a statue. Afraid to move. We're close enough that I can feel his heartbeat, or maybe that's mine, pulsing with reckless abandon.

Phil moves me backward across the floor as he

follows Kit's cues. I can't look up at him. It's like he's the sun during an eclipse and I'll go blind with one look.

"Now pivot. Lead with your hips."

I'm not even sure what he means, but it doesn't matter because Phil's holding me tight enough so my body has no choice but to follow him. He's carrying all the weight of this lesson while I'm treading water in the deep end and my lifeguard is tall, dark, and handsome.

"And now," Kit sings the words. "Follow us in the ocho pattern."

And just like that, we're doing figure eights around the studio.

After our next pivot, I squint at Phil. "There's no way this is your first time doing the tango. You've had lessons!" He shakes his head. "Then you watched a lot of Youtube videos!"

"Guilty as charged." His smile has enough wattage to light the entire studio.

Kit stops for a second and looks at us. "And here I thought I was going to have to get out the ladder."

"The ladder?" I ask. "Why on earth would we need a ladder?"

"To get to the next level, of course."

Phil lets out a deep laugh, which makes Kitty giggle. I can't help myself; for a second I forget what I'm doing and where I am.

It's like the first taste of ice cream on a summer day. Turning on the Christmas lights. Sinking into a warm bath. I've missed this. The touch of a man and the spontaneous shared laughter. The joy of being part of a couple. My shoulders relax and I think I stop sweating.

"Where are you two off to next?" asks Kit.

Kitty purrs and reality bites back. Going out in public with Phil Young cannot happen.

As if on cue, the song slows and I drop Phil's hand from mine.

Somehow, between the handcuffs and whip and then Phil showing up, I forgot about my plan to go over to The Old Owl after our lesson. Shit.

"Oh, nowhere!" I look at my wrist, forgetting my watch isn't there. "I have to get home."

Phil puts his hands in his pockets and bounces back and forth on his heels. "It'd be a shame to end this night so early. How about a drive?"

A drive? So we can neck in the woods?

"You'll be just like the teenagers," says Kitty.

A maniacal laugh rings through my head, but judging from everyone's faces, it's not just in my mind.

I have got to put an end to this night. My phone pings, and then everyone else's does. The universe finally answered my prayers with a diversion.

Kit is the first to draw his out, and he reads aloud, "Emergency town meeting, tomorrow night, 7 p.m."

All our phones buzz again. This time there's a message from GG.

Islanders,

It's anyone's guess what's got the mayor's undies in a knot! Could it be the rumor that's running rampant that whomever is renting the Harris home is in hiding after an unseemly TikTok swinging scandal? Or maybe we're barking up the wrong tree and it's something else entirely. Only time will tell! See you at 7.

xoxo,

GG

Have I been saved? Or have I been caught?

NEED MORE HOUSEWIVES?

Read more about the Housewives here!

ACKNOWLEDGMENTS

Oh my goodness! You've made it to the end of book four. Can you believe it? It feels surreal to be wrapping up the Sherman family's adventures at the same time my last two kids are getting ready to leave for college. Maybe that's why finishing this book felt a little more emotional.

Do you ever get to the end of a book and immediately flip to the acknowledgements, hoping for a peek behind the curtain? I do. I read every name, wondering who they are and what part they played. Because even after reading fiction, you can't help but feel like you know the person who wrote it.

That's exactly why my kids don't want to read my books—or so they say. They see themselves and our lives tucked into the pages—sometimes more obviously than others. Even though Greensea is made up, it's stitched together with pieces of the real world: conversations overheard, places I love, memories, daydreams, and the chaos and beauty of our ordinary everyday life.

So thank you for loving Greensea. For ferrying over again and again. For finding the magic in this island and its people. It means more than I can ever say. And don't worry, this isn't the end of Greensea...the spotlight is just shifting away from the Shermans.

Thank you to all my favorite local shops for cheering me on, especially my bookstore besties, Bittina and Kevin at *Away With Words*. Your encouragement keeps me afloat.

I'm lucky to be part of such a vibrant writing community—at BARN and beyond. Writing can be lonely, but you've made it a shared adventure. Huge thanks to Jenna for all the tweaking, Audrey for editing, and to my mom and Gill for your ongoing support and sharp proofreading eyes.

Thanks to all my lovely friends supporting me on the reformer, the courts, the walking trails, and all around town.

Jen—what would I do without you? Business partner, cover designer, editor, proofreader, and most importantly, dear friend—this venture is nothing without you. And now we've started a new venture as Liz and Jess. Love uncovering new adventures with you!

Finally, thanks to my fam for being a constant source of inspiration and support. You guys go above and beyond giving me material. I love all of you more than you'll ever know. A special thanks to Justin for supporting my fictional worlds.

xoxo,

julie

ABOUT THE AUTHOR

Julie Farley loves writing books filled with big families, lots of heart, and plenty of laughs. She lives on an island in the Pacific Northwest with her husband and four amazing kids. Julie has a bachelor's degree from the University of Notre Dame and a graduate degree from DePaul University. When she's not busy with her family or writing books, you'll find her watching reality TV...of any sort!

ABOUT FOG HOUSE PRESS

Fog House Press is an independent boutique publishing company offering authors a comprehensive suite of services to ensure their work shines. Our mission is to empower authors to tell their best story by providing full professional publishing services, as well as a host of individual offerings.

ALSO BY JULIE FARLEY

A Greensea Island Adventure Series

Love Songs and Ferry Tales

Cozy Cabins and Ferry Tales

Fake Dates and Ferry Tales

Best Friends and Ferry Tales

The New Ever After Series

Tripped Up Love

The New Ever After

Another Tomorrow

Sunny Valley Girls (Liz Fields and Jess Lynne)

Big Waves Down Under

Holed Up In Jackson

A Fling in the Wild

Behind Two Palms